To my lovely niece
Love Aunt Gwen
2018

Little Wave

By Gwen C. Delp

Forward

The Oregon coastline in the far west of the United States is a national treasure. The beaches are wide and windy, with forests for their back yards. The green of the trees contrasted with the silver and blue ocean is stunning. There are huge rock formations, tide pools, rocky bays with crashing waves, whales and seals and sea lions. Seabirds scurry in the tide, and pelicans and gulls fly overhead. Beautiful homes dot the coastline with remote driveways that lead up tree-lined roads to the perches only the rich can enjoy. The towns have shops and restaurants filled with shells and seafood. People come with their families and enjoy the beautiful Pacific and its wild yet peaceful scenery. They stay in the quaint cottages and the luxurious resorts. They leave their lives behind for a day or a week.

But there is another side to that coastline. It lies across the highway and up in the valleys that roll into the Pacific. Poverty and decay are part of that landscape. There are fisheries that are reaching extinction, forests that are over logged. Shops open and close like the setting sun. Seagull marauders are everywhere and their white waste splats on every street.

You need only open your eyes and you can see the working class, some stripped of purpose or just scraping out a living in the sand and salty air. The rusted-out pickups and cars, the yards littered with old fishing nets and driftwood. Not everyone who lives there is represented in this tale, but a rougher seam of humanity runs through all beach towns. This side of the coastline, the other side of the highway – that is where this story comes from. That is where these characters live.

"It is not true. Life is not slain by death.

The vast, immortal sea shall have her own,

Shall garner to her this expiring breath,

Shall reap where she has sown."

On the monument at Depot Bay, Oregon

Chapter 1

The End

How did she end up here again? She felt his hand tight on her wrist, pushing her down the path. She tried to turn and face him, but he jerked her back around.

He smelled like whiskey and cigarettes. He had empty black eyes and pocked skin, and his hoodie was frayed, boots scuffed with sand and mud. He was not that different from any of the other scum she had encountered.

She saw the edge of the cliff, heard the surf pounding far below. The air was full of salty mist, and it stung her eyes. She had never been this far. Fists, knives, guns, those she had seen. She had scars, but that was all about intimidation. This guy was about action. He stood behind her so calm. No shaking, no talking, very strong. She twisted, but she was trapped.

Suddenly he spun her around and looked at her face to face. He said, "I don't know you; I don't care about you, but you won't stop them from fucking you up. You are a weak bitch."

She was not afraid of pain, and she was not afraid to die. Falling backwards was her only fear; she had always wanted to look straight into the wind.

As he pushed her over the edge, she saw his long black hair blowing and him tucking it behind his ear. She knew he would light a cigarette and walk away.

Chapter 2

Leah

There was one apartment that was on top of a garage. It was two rooms. One had a shower and a toilet. The other had everything else. It was one of my favorites. There was a window that looked out at the Malcolms' back yard and kitchen window. It was their garage we were living in.

Sometimes I hid in the closet when Mrs. Malcolm came in to find Lou Ann and get the rent. She wasn't there. Mrs. Malcolm opened drawers, checked under the bed, even the closet, but I was small and curled up on a side shelf with a suitcase in front of me.

Lou Ann told me we couldn't stay there anymore. The Malcolms wanted me to go to school. Her hair was up in a loose bun, and the bruise on her left cheek was green and purple. A cigarette was smoking in the ashtray and the card table we used for everything was covered with beer cans and plastic red cups. Home. We left in the middle of the night.

Then there was the apartment in the basement of the Smoke Shop, dark and smelly like mildew and tobacco. We had to go up the stairs and use the employee bathroom. We had a sink in the room where we washed everything from cups to our bodies.

The guy who owned the Smoke Shop was one of the more brutal men Lou Ann encountered. He never even acknowledged I was alive. He would open the door to the cellar and shout, "Lou Ann, get up here!" If she was there, she would stub out her cigarette, smooth back her hair and tell me if she wasn't back by dark I could go to 7-11 and steal some food. She never came back before dark. She didn't even know how I ate some of the time.

There were several spots I knew. Behind the diner, there was a dumpster I would jump in. My favorite find was French fries. You had to rip open the bags, but there was always something that was edible. I was used to the smell of the dumpster. It smelled like dinner.

Then there was a small grocery store that had a loose chain-link fence. I could squeeze in and walk right into the storeroom most nights. Chips, Twinkies, warm Pepsi, candy bars… Quiet like a little rat, slipping in and out.

She usually showed up about 9:00 a.m. Sometimes she had been beaten, sometimes she had some cuts on her arms. Once a hunk of her hair was gone. She never said anything, and I never asked. I didn't know anything but the rules she had made clear to me at some point in our life together. They included: don't ask questions, stay quiet when you are told, hide from other adults when I am not around.

Sometimes there was money. We would go to Denny's for pancakes. She would brush my hair and braid it and dig around trying to find me clean clothes. I don't know where the clothes came from. They were always used and all different sizes. She always put the blue things on me, to match my eyes. She had a way of tying up a t-shirt or belting on a skirt and I thought I looked great.

I had no desires, no dreams. My world was her. No other children, no school, just her in varying degrees of dishevelment. She seemed to love me, and she wanted to keep me. I knew I was not supposed to be with her, so I didn't talk to anyone.

She was pretty. To live the life she had chosen, you had to have some appeal. She was shapely, but a little boney. Her hair was always strawberry blonde, and it was for real – no dye. She had very light blue eyes and soft freckles. She had a "big rack," as I heard Aunt Sharon say, and "it gave her nothing but heartache."

Some of the men were kind for several months. She would have some jewelry (which we hawked) and some amazing underwear. Once a guy named Butch got her a white leather coat and knee-high white leather boots. She had a lot of money then, but one day she came home barefoot without the boots or the coat and a broken jaw. She put on other clothes and told me to stay put. She came back with her jaw wired shut. We stayed in the apartment for a long time. We played cards, and she ordered me pizza while she drank beer and milk. Then the money ran out.

That's when we went to Uncle Carl. I had never seen him. I didn't know he existed. Lou Ann was not the type to share information. He was a big guy, dark hair, muscles, tall. He had a quiet way about him, but I could tell he was really angry at Lou Ann. Carl winked at me and was kind to me from the moment I met him. But he looked at Lou Ann with what I learned later in life was an expression of love and hate. I understood it because I felt it too; I just didn't have a name for it.

My first impression of Uncle Carl and Aunt Sharon's house was how big it was. It had so many rooms and porches and grass. I felt overwhelmed. Uncle Carl would find me in the closet in the room I shared with Lou Ann. He coaxed me out with candy. Aunt Sharon was tougher. She said, "You can hide but you cannot disappear, little girl."

Sharon wanted to take me to school. She spent some time talking to Lou Ann about it. Lou Ann was freaked out and said it would be a disaster. I really didn't know what school would be like or if I wanted to go. I just knew that Aunt Sharon was strong, and Lou Ann didn't win every conversation with her.

Sharon was a bustling woman. She moved fast and steady on her feet. Her hair was kinky and salt and pepper, and it was knotted on top of her head. I watched her make the knot; no hair pins. She did it fast, like she did everything. She was plump but not flabby. She wore the same uniform every day— pull on jeans, running shoes, a flowered blouse: short sleeve in winter, sleeveless in summer.

She was a woman without illusions. She did not find anyone to be particularly interesting. Everyone was just what they were; she was just Sharon, no pretense.

When she brushed my tangled hair the second day I was there (she caught me in the hallway), she wedged me between her knees, sitting on the bed. She was gentle, but quickly my tangled brown hair was in two solid braids down my back. She kissed the top of my head as I wiggled free. That became her signature affection for me from then on, a kiss on the top of the head.

Lou Ann was restless. She paced and smoked in the backyard. She looked like a skeleton in her shorts and bikini top. Her scars were still there. Some were white lines; one was on the cheekbone that never healed right. I watched her from the kitchen tables as I ate piles of pancakes, peanut butter and jelly sandwiches, chocolate layer cake, and gallons of milk.

Aunt Sharon thought I was a mess. Soon she started taking over my care. I had not really had care, just survival and time with Lou Ann when she wasn't scrambling to feed us and whatever else she did. I didn't know what attention was, but I knew I was getting something new at this house. It felt good but somewhat overwhelming. Sometimes I hid just to get away from it, the caring. Sometimes I felt afraid and alone, even more than when my care was minimal. I started to realize my life with Lou Ann was a mess.

Carla was my age and she lived close by. Aunt Sharon introduced her to me. She was a chubby little blonde girl with a lisp, and she always wore dresses. She giggled all the time and talked about things I did not understand. Now I know she loved fairy tales and princesses. I didn't understand her, but I liked her. She seemed simple, and she didn't ask questions. My silence was not important to her because she had so many silly things to talk about. I didn't really play with Carla. I really had no concept of how to play with her. Mostly, I just observed Carla.

I had grown up very fast; in fact, I cannot remember when childhood ended for me, as I am vaguely aware it never existed. Trying to befriend another child was awkward. She was put into my world like a prop. I was supposed to want this in my life, but really, I didn't need it. But it was expected, so I played along.

Aunt Sharon was very smart. She saw everything, and I am sure she planned all my experiences with care, including Carla. I wasn't used to large grocery stores. I had only been to small corner stores. I knew how to steal a carton of milk and escape with two of Lou Ann's favorite beers, but shopping for groceries in a cart and paying for them with a plastic card had never been a part of my world.

Aunt Sharon said, "Hang on to the grocery cart and stay put." The cart was huge, and she filled it full. She explained what she put in and why. I learned about eggs and lettuce. I wanted the cookies in packages, but she bought chocolate chips and brown sugar. The volume was overwhelming to me. The food was heavenly.

My skinny body became rounded, and my lank hair was shiny and thicker. I did not know I was unhealthy before. Now I kept touching my arms and legs in amazement. They were fuller and softer. I knew it was Aunt Sharon's care, but it was still a little disconnected in my brain. What was happening to me?

One day Lou Ann screamed at Aunt Sharon. I was in the kitchen having an egg salad sandwich. I was sitting in my usual spot, close to the back door. Lou Ann had been acting stranger than ever the past few days. She was jittery, and she smoked non-stop. She burst through the back door and screamed that I was being turned into a fat, stupid kid. I was losing my edge. How could I survive? "What if you throw us away, Sharon? What if I die? She is too soft – stop feeding her. She needs to be tough!"

Then she started crying. It was wailing, sobbing, screaming, behavior that I had not seen before. Aunt Sharon seemed unmoved. She kept cutting up vegetables. I backed up the stairs and headed to my closet. I could still hear her, but it was better. Aunt Sharon said, "Lou Ann, get a grip. Destroy yourself but stop with the kid." Lou Ann's sobs were quieter, and I heard Aunt Sharon's kitchen radio click on. End of the day's drama.

When Lou Ann and I moved, when we were on our own, there were no "things" we moved from place to place. She used a grocery sack or garbage bag to pack. We left most things behind, like clothes or pots and pans. I thought it was normal.

Aunt Sharon and Uncle Carl had so many things. I had never felt towels like theirs. The soaps and shampoos and the lotion... Candles burning for no reason but to smell good. Smells were everywhere. Lou Ann smelled like she always had: cigarettes and lipstick.

Once I got used to it, I loved showering. When I was told I had to do it every day, I was quietly thrilled. Clear warm water falling over me and shampoo that smelled like coconuts and pink soap and lotion when I got out, wow.

The first one I took, Aunt Sharon sent me back in twice with instructions to scrub harder. The wash rags turned black. I didn't know how to wash at first, but Sharon taught me. Head and hair first, then upper body and work your way down. Soap up with the wash rag; don't be afraid to scrub. When I stepped out, I tingled from head to toe and buried my face in the sweet-smelling towel.

———————————

All those first months Lou Ann was a jittery smoking mess. She would not eat meals. She grabbed snacks and fussed over her weight. She looked skinny, and next to Aunt Sharon I saw her coloring was gray. The lightly freckled skin was pale, and there were black bags under her eyes. She sat in the back yard with Uncle Carl and they talked in low voices. His focus was Lou Ann, and Aunt Sharon's focus was me.

No one said how long or why we were here. I was too scared to ask. I felt attached to Lou Ann, but I was seeing what she could not do for me. I did not want to leave. I wanted Lou Ann to eat and sit and talk to me and stay here so we could feel safe all of the time. But Lou Ann was not someone who was looking for a safe place. She didn't understand "safe," and I don't think she believed anything was safe. Safe made her edgy. I couldn't help her.

I didn't ask questions the first few months I lived with Carl and Sharon. I was not used to conversation, and I didn't even know what I could ask. I was suspended in a world of sweet smells, fresh clothes, and good food. But I knew Lou Ann well enough to know she could decide to go at any time, and I didn't know if Sharon would let her take me. So, you see, I was not really feeling "safe" either.

Chapter 3

Sharon

Imagine a girl, just turning the corner to puberty. Her hair whacked off on the ends, down to her mid-back. Dull and tangled and hastily pulled back into a pony tail. Her skin was grayish and there were dark circles under her eyes. Her fingernails were broken and dirty. Her feet were uncared for with rough patches and broken toenails.

Her clothes were ill-fitting and strangely put together. The first time she walked in our door, she wore blue fleece pajama bottoms, dirty and worn thin. She had on a dress that was for a small woman, a shirtwaist, cinched at the waist with an old blue fleece tie, like you would find on a bathrobe. Her shoes were old white Converse sneakers, ripped and ragged.

She smelled of cigarettes, body odor, and mildew. Underneath the layers of neglect, she was beautiful. She was quiet and watchful. She looked at me with a flicker of hope in her extraordinary blue eyes. She knew she needed help, but not what that might be.

There were other clothes in the black garbage bag that Lou Ann tossed on the bedroom floor. All of the things for Leah were blue, and none of them were fit to wear. I washed them all, but the smells of mildew and smoke stayed deep in the fabric, like it was woven into their lives.

The showers and shampoo helped steam away the filth from her skin. Brushing, trimming and braiding, lotion, clipping, and good food. Simple but never given. She was a little ghost child emerging from layers of dirt and grime; that was how it was with Leah.

Lou Ann did not comment on the changes I was making. She knew full well when she brought her here things would change. That was her plan. But she never commented on any of it. She stayed uninterested in Leah's physical state. I thought she was a shit mother and found it hard not to slap her.

Chapter 4

Lou Ann

When I went to Carl for help I was broken. Too many falls to the bottom. And Leah, she was getting too big to keep hiding. I knew he would be angry. There was nothing more or less to expect in that department. Leah would not be easy for him to understand. Maybe he had heard about her; it's possible, but not certain. I didn't know his old lady. I would be a big surprise to her. She would be angry too.

But anger was not my real concern. Turning Leah over to them, that had to happen. I needed to be sure they could handle it. I just didn't give a shit if they were mad at me. I knew how that felt, and it had never stopped me before.

Carl had made a life, even with all the shit in our past. He could handle this kid; I just knew it. I had to take her there because it was all there was to do. He would not turn his back on us. He still loved me, I was sure. Anyway, I hoped he did.

He met us at a gas station. We climbed into the truck. He had never seen Leah. The shock on his face flashed to anger, then he pulled away from the curb with us. I knew I lost Leah right then. I knew it before I called him at the pay phone.

Chapter 5

Carl

My fucking sister. Gone for twelve years, dead for all I knew and now she was here. She had a little girl. What a sad mess of a kid. Dirty tangled hair, a wilding. She didn't say much. She could be as still as a piece of furniture.

I kept thinking of a feral cat that Lou Ann tamed when we lived in the big brick house in Astoria. She spent hours offering scraps and water and sitting on the steps waiting. The cat was scrawny and had a horrible sore on its back…she didn't give up.

It looked like Lou Ann had been beaten a lot. She refused to tell me anything about it. She was the same mess she was the last time I saw her, the last time my mother saw her.

She was only seventeen then. She just walked away from the house in flip flops, shorts and a bikini top. She had a pack of cigarettes stuck in her waistband and nothing else. Mom was passed out on the kitchen floor. I was in Coos Bay on a boat working for Joe Gunner. One of the neighbors told May they saw her leave that way with nothing, not even a purse. Lou Ann was always crazy like that. No plan, no fear, just moving.

Sometimes guys would tell me they saw her in Long Beach or Seaside. I followed up on leads for a while, but I really did not have time. I was working long hours on fishing boats, hard physical work. And my mother still needed help. Part of me knew Lou Ann wasn't going to accept any help from me anyway. I was all part of the ugliness of her childhood. I didn't try very hard to find her.

One time we got a postcard at Mom's before she drank herself to death. Lou Ann sent it from Hawaii. It had a picture of a hula girl on it and it read:

> *If you are still alive, May*
>
> *I am in Paradise*
>
> *If you are still alive, May*
>
> *Stay away from Alaskans*
>
> *Lou Ann*

I don't think she had Leah yet, but I am not sure. The kid was off the grid. No birth certificate, medical records, no last name as far as we knew. Lou Ann said she was about twelve, and she just called her Leah. She was not sure of her birthday. Fuckin' Lou Ann.

Sharon was pragmatic about it. I don't think Lou Ann was of much interest to her. She grew up in a house of women and chaos. She made it through. She was zoned in on Leah. I knew how Sharon operated. This would be slow and steady work. Leah would become as strong as she could be and as smart as she could be. Sharon was not talking about it. She was just doing it.

Lou Ann was my problem. What could I do for her but feed her? I thought she was strung out when I picked her up, but it wasn't that. She was just crazy and like a wild animal. No taming her, but it's the letting go of Leah she was struggling with. Who knows what she thought she would do? Keep her? God knows where and no school, no family, no life. That fucking Lou Ann…

Chapter 6

Lou Ann

I tried to get Carl to hit me. I just needed it. He wouldn't do it. I even said, "You're not your father's kid. You are a puss. Just hit me; you'll feel better, little boy." He looked at me, and I was sickened by his pity. I wanted that version of our old man. Kick the shit out of a woman, break a bone, yank her hair. Cocksucker, just do it.

But Carl walked back in the house. Through the kitchen window I saw him wrap his arms around Sharon and kiss her. He is really not his father's kid. He is a made-up man in his made-up house with his solid wife. Why in the hell did I come here? These people are living a fantasy.

Maybe they can't handle taking care of Leah. Maybe they are just too soft, too sentimental. They will need raw gut to see her through what I have put her through. Yeah, it won't be a walk in the park, but they are all I have got, all that Leah needs. There was no other alternative but start pimping her out and that wasn't happenin'. She was not walking that path.

Chapter 7

Sharon

Lou Ann could not keep Leah, but we had to get her legally. She needed to see a doctor, go to school, see a dentist, so much to do. But first I had to get her used to living here. Get her used to a normal life. I could not send her to school yet.

I had to keep Lou Ann for a while, but Carl was going to suffer when she left, and he was suffering while she stayed. No win for him. She would never stay.

She was just a myth before she came. That whole family, I never met any of them. When I found Carl, I was not looking. He was drinking heavy at a bar in Newport. I was working behind the bar. It was a dirty fishermen's bar, but I could make enough to eat and rent a small room.

Carl was handsome and hard, young and sad. It was a short courtship. We needed each other. We were both willing. No romance, but there was something. We recognized each other, like we had been waiting.

He made enough money that I stopped working. I cooked enough that he stopped drinking. We had good sex. We paid the bills. Neither one of us had ever had all that before. We felt good, peaceful.

This Lou Ann business brought up things for Carl. We had never gone too deep into our pasts. They were tangled and dark. It was there in our eyes, our voices, even the way we made love. But we had left it alone.

Carl seemed obsessed and yet repulsed by his sister. I just watched because it was his battle to fight. But Leah, she was the victim, and I had to teach her how to stop being one. She was a good project.

She was starting to respond.

Chapter 8

Lou Ann

Our mother was named May. She was small and had long black hair. She looked like an Indian, but she never would say. She was always cooking and drying fish. Our whole house smelled of fish, cigarettes, and whiskey.

She drank all the years I lived at home. She drank straight whiskey. She could work hard on our lot and cook fish, all the time saturated in whiskey.

Sometimes she took us to the beach where she would walk with a piece of driftwood for a walking stick, and then she would sit and look at the ocean and sip more whiskey while we played on the logs and wandered wherever we pleased for hours. She called me Little Wave because I ran in and out of the surf. She called Carl Boy Bear. We were happy then.

She wore her hair in a long braid down her back. She wore little cotton dresses she had sewn – one pattern, a shift. She liked plain colors: red, blue, green and brown. She had a leather belt she wore around her waist with a silver buckle shaped like an owl.

He beat her with that belt. She never cried out; she just crawled into another room and barricaded the door. That's when Carl and I would run: rain, snow, summer heat. We were fast, and we knew where to go. One of our favorite places was Granny Parsons' house. It was a good ten-minute run, but the back door was unlocked, and it was dry in there. Her kitchen was all white and blue, and her donuts were homemade and sugary. She was quiet and no questions. We loved her.

We could not get away from our father every time. He was determined, and sometimes he would get us in his grip. He was hardest on me. He hated me. He said I was a stray cat. He slapped me, punched me, and as soon as he could, he raped me. He waited for me to look like a woman. Somewhere in the sick mind of Earl, that made it okay. I wasn't his daughter and I wasn't a little child, so it was fine, his male right. That is what he said to me.

He would wait until May passed out for the night. He always waited until Carl was gone playing sports, practices, etc. It wasn't any use to cry out. It was rough and quick, and he ended it by hitting my bare bottom and pushing me out of the bedroom he shared with May. May snored on the kitchen floor. I washed up and crawled into my bed with silent sobs. By thirteen I was smoking Camels and staying quiet. I was scared and ashamed and I didn't want anyone to know, most of all Carl.

I hated the old man, but I hated May too. They were useless to Carl and me. We made our way without them most of the time. It was fucking hard.

Granny Parsons kept us sometimes for a week or more. She had a bunk bed in her back bedroom. There were wagon train lamps on the dresser and end table, and the blankets were scratchy, but no one hurt us.

Sometimes she would leave, and we knew she went to check on May. She never brought her to the house beat up, but we knew she was taking care of her.

She was not our Granny. She had other grandkids, and if they came when we were there we played, but we had to go home to sleep.

We still wanted to go home for a long time. I wanted my mother, even when she was crippled up with alcohol. I wanted her to kiss the top of my head and smooth my hair back. I wanted her to ask me if I was feeling okay. I wanted her to breath in my smell and say, "Something isn't right here. You smell like Earl."

They are both dead and gone, now. Good riddance, I say.

Chapter 9

Leah

The neighbor girl, Carla, was running out of stuff to talk about, I guess. Now she was pestering me about my life. "Where did you used to live? How come I never saw you before? Why don't you go to school? Where is your dad? How old are you? Where were you born?"

I knew how to steal, but I didn't really understand lying, and I knew I didn't have any answers for her. But I could play poker. So, Carla learned too. She was a very slow learner, but she liked playing with lemon drops for chips (Sharon's idea). I let her win as much as seemed reasonable. She was so ridiculous and silly and besides she loved lemon drops.

Carla liked to make plastic bead necklaces. They were awful. I received one as a present almost every week. She had a weird sense of color, and nothing she made really matched. I tried to tell her I liked blue, but it was almost like she did the opposite and every necklace she gave me lacked even one blue bead. Sharon said I should give her something because it was obvious she liked to give, so she probably liked to receive. I was not very crafty, but I decided to try making her some cookies. Sharon was all excited about this and she helped me select a recipe and watched over my shoulder as I tried out a complex pinwheel cookie.

You had to divide sugar cookie dough into two parts and flavor one part chocolate. Then you rolled the dough into thin sheets and stacked them. Then you rolled it up like a cinnamon roll and cut them in uniform slices. It took full concentration and no whining, which is what Sharon said when I complained that my arms were tired from stirring and rolling. The dough was delicious, and I wanted to suggest we just cut out flat cookies. But Sharon wasn't going to let me do this halfway. I was going to experience the full drama of baking fancy cookies and that was that!

Sharon had shown me how to take a shoe box and wrap the bottom in wrapping paper and then wrap the top separately so you could take the lid off. I chose some birthday paper we had with pink and yellow roses on it. Then we lined the box with foil. It was pretty awesome, and Carla seemed to be very pleased. I didn't think anyone could get that happy over a box of cookies. But then, she started eating them, and I got upset. She was practically shoving them in her mouth. I wanted to slap her hand and tell her that was hours of work I had just put into making them and could she just enjoy one slowly.

Later I told Sharon how that made me feel and she laughed. She taught me something then that I have never forgotten. She said a person needs to learn to give gifts and walk away. Your part is done once you hand it to the other person. Whatever they do with it is no longer your business. They can use it, lose it, break it, give it away, gobble it up, or forget to say thank you. You need to remember the joy you felt in the process of giving. You do not get to choose what the receiver feels. Because I didn't have much experience in giving at the time she shared this thought with me, I was able to take Sharon's advice and use it. I did not turn into a great giver, but when I do, I know what my part is in the exchange.

I went to Carla's house just once. Her mom insisted I come for dinner. I did not want to go. I did not know if I could pull it off, if there would be questions from her mother, and I didn't want to eat anyone's food but Sharon's. The visit did not go well. Her dad had a big, booming voice and he talked during the entire meal. We had something I did not recognize, and her little brother made faces at me all through dinner. Her mom kept looking at me with this pitying smile and shaking her head. Carla just gobbled up her food, slurped her milk and then farted. She got in trouble from her big-mouth dad for that, and it scared the crap out of me. Carla didn't seem to listen to him, and when dessert came it was ice cream made with goat's milk, and I choked when I tasted it. Carla's little brat brother was allergic to cow's milk. I could not leave fast enough. Carla asked me to come again and I said,

"No thanks. I cannot eat any food but Sharon's." She just shrugged her shoulders and asked me what my favorite food was or my favorite movie.

Food, I knew: warm Pepsi and a bag of Doritos from the old life, pancakes from the new one. But movies, I hadn't seen any yet. I had watched some television at Aunt Sharon's for the first time. I like *Tom and Jerry*, but I just got sad sometimes for Tom. He seemed so stupid.

My favorite thing was the radio. Aunt Sharon liked rock-n-roll, and we listened to all of it, old and new. If it was Tom Petty, we would turn it up really loud, and she would sing along; knew every word. She said if she could make dinner for Tom Petty, it would be pot roast, potatoes and gravy and a fresh peach pie.

Sometimes I felt Sharon watching me. I felt her eyes on me. No one had ever really looked at me in my other life. Men with Lou Ann mostly ignored me. Shopkeepers didn't see me, as I knew how to blend in. Waitresses, the few times we saw them, were kind but busy. Sometimes Lou Ann would stare at me, but it was not me she was looking at. It usually meant we were moving. She always got quiet right before a move. Then things moved fast: the escape, the search for shelter, the long periods of time alone that followed.

Just one time we went to a place with other women. We were in Portland. Lou Ann said, "You are going to be a mute. This means you cannot talk. I will talk for you. Promise me." I did.

At that time Lou Ann had a broken nose that she had tried to set herself. Her eyes were black and blue, and her upper lip was split. The shelter let us in. They set Lou Ann's nose properly. We got two cots, two hot meals, a shared shower room and a room with books. Lou Ann had taught me to read, and I tried out some harder ones than the newspapers I pulled out of trash cans. I read a book called *Blue Petunia* about a girl who grew up on a farm and had a pet pig. When we left, I took it with me. I read it over and over. I liked the garden description and the wash on the line. Aunt Sharon's house came close.

Chapter 10

Sharon

Lou Ann had taught her to read. It was just amazing. She could read anything. I asked her to read me articles from the paper when I baked bread. She had good pronunciation and cadence. She paused appropriately and changed her tone to match the mood of the story.

I asked her if she wanted to go to a library. Like many things, she hesitated. She wasn't sure what it would be like or if she knew how to do it.

Our first trip to get her some clothes was very hard on her. She had no idea what to do. All she wanted were blue things, and she was not willing to try things on. When it came to shoes, I picked out blue and white polka-dotted Keds. I measured her foot. She could not quit smiling when I handed her the bag to carry. She loved them. She wore them down to breakfast in her blue and white pajamas every day.

Her eyes are blue, but not the pale blue of Lou Ann's. Carl's eyes are dark brown, like chocolate drops. But Leah's are deep blue, and they look like shattered glass. They are striking and large. They fit in her little heart-shaped face with rosebud lips. She doesn't look like Lou Ann at all. She is her own exquisite self.

Lou Ann said she was Leah's mother, but Leah always called her Lou Ann. They seemed like sisters to me, bound to one another, but they were their own women, separate, alone together.

Carl watched Leah. I could see the love in his eyes. But he was wary and didn't give her too much attention when Lou Ann was in the room. We all knew Leah would stay. We all knew Lou Ann would go, but Carl wanted to keep her as long as he could. Sometimes I didn't know why, but other times I felt it too. I wanted Lou Ann to stay, even though I thought she was a ridiculous woman. She had that thing about her. You could not get enough of it, whatever it was.

I have siblings, somewhere. I had a mother, but Carl is all I claim now. I never longed for what I didn't have or even the relationships from the past. I closed those doors for good. But now I think I will have Leah. I want her.

Chapter 11

Carl

Lou Ann needed a job. When I told her, she laughed and told me she had one. I told her you cannot keep it up; you are too old. She cackled and said, "I am only thirty, Carl."

I could not find the words I needed to tell her that her life was killing her because she was on a suicide mission. If I had kicked her out and kept Leah, she would have just died quicker.

She was a trapped animal. She wanted to get out of the cage and start the hunt again. But she loved Leah enough to gnaw at her ropes a while longer.

One day she asked why our father said she was a stray. I looked at her in amazement. All this life experience, and she couldn't see it? My eyes are brown, and my hair is black, like May's. I am built like our old man, strong and tall. Lou Ann is my age, exactly, the same birthday even. Strawberry blonde hair, pale blue eyes, freckles... What the hell? Did no one ever tell her? (I thought Granny Parsons told her. Wasn't Lou Ann there that day? She had to have been there. I knew that Granny knew she was not their biological child.)

Lou Ann was holding her cigarette in her long thin hand, shaky with broken nails. She was like a lost child then, with the light of the sun through the leaves lighting up strands of her hair. Her battle-worn body was still good, but there were so many war wounds. I said, "Our old man was an asshole, just forget it."

She looked like she had already moved on to another thought. She just stared into the distance.

Lou Ann doesn't know that I know what happened to her at my father's hands. Her mind is a mosaic, and jagged edges keep the pieces apart. I wanted to tell her that I wanted to save her. I wanted to talk about his death and how she didn't do it. I did it.

But her concentration came and went. Conversations were choppy, and I don't know if she was able to really think. I thought it was some kind of defense. God, I didn't even know what all she had been through for the past twelve years. I couldn't judge.

Sharon and I talked a little about the future, but she didn't push me. We both knew Lou Ann brought us Leah. That was why she came. Now we just needed to figure out how to handle it.

Lou Ann kept saying Leah had to be tough. She worried we were spoiling her. Shit, we were just feeding her, clothing her and giving her a home. We didn't have lots of money and besides, Leah didn't ask for anything, not one thing, for a long time. I thought she was tough enough.

Leah had no concept of her beauty. She had no idea what most girls her age were doing. She was a wilding; she was able to be so still and fade into her surroundings. I had no idea what made her tick. I could only imagine. We didn't even know how we could spoil her. Her only thrill appeared to be showers and food.

Sharon said she smelled everything all the time. She smelled her clothes before she slipped them on. She smelled her sheets. She smelled the hairbrush. She touched everything, but very lightly.

But when I sat down and played poker with her, she beat me solid, over and over. She didn't seem to care about winning. She just did it like it was easy.

She was a mystery. She was here, and we needed to keep her.

Chapter 12

Leah

Once Lou Ann had a real job as a waitress. We had a trailer, tiny like a camper. The owner of the diner rented it to us; one day's wages per month. Lou Ann wore a uniform. It was tight in the chest, but I liked seeing her in it. Every night we were together. We ate diner food, and she taught me to play poker.

We were in Seaside, so when she worked I could wander around on the beach. If anyone asked why I wasn't in school I told them I was home-schooled, per Lou Ann's instructions.

I knew Lou Ann would not be able to go for too long without a man. I knew she wanted the pain. I thought things like, this is how strawberry blondes are, or all women want that sometimes. Deep down I think I knew she was really messed up. But she was all I knew.

She met a guy who was nice. He had a pickup, and we drove to dinner in it twice. He ordered me a hamburger with fries. Lou Ann basically ate lettuce. He held her hand and stroked her hair. He called her Lola, and he bought her a new coat. He patted my head and sent me downtown for candy so they could be alone. It was a short relationship. He got too serious and actually wanted us to move in with him. But worse offense, I would be sent to school.

No bruises, no broken bones – she dumped him. No problem for me. I did not attach to anyone.

We were there several months, but I knew Lou Ann. We would need to leave soon. She was smoking more, pacing. She missed work and then one night she went out. I saw her put on a red bra and a shredded tank top. Her jeans were tight, and she put on high heels. Two nights out and she came back with a split lip and a shiner.

I put my few clothes in the garbage bag, and we walked away. She had bus fare, so we went to Lincoln City. I missed my little bed in the trailer, but Lou Ann found us an old abandoned cabin. Once we got the mice shit off my cot, it was okay.

Chapter 13

Sharon

She started to leave at night. The first time she sauntered out the back door with thick makeup, hair pulled up and tight jeans. She turned and looked back at the house and flipped her cigarette into the alley. Leah and I were upstairs in my room putting clean clothes away. Leah stood at the window until Lou Ann was gone. Then, without any expression, she went back to hanging up Carl's shirts.

Leah was a good companion. She was quiet, and when she talked, her voice was soft. She imitated all my movements. She could make beds, slice vegetables, fluff pillows, scrub the sink. She was like a little sponge soaking up my world of domesticity.

I waited for more questions and more answers. Her shell was not so hard as it was strong. It seemed like she was made of hard glass – light in and out, but no cracks.

She didn't cry out loud. She didn't laugh, but she smiled often. One day she picked some fall mums from the garden and brought them in and arranged them in a water glass. She asked if they could be in their room. When I went to bring towels, they were on the nightstand. A little house woman in the making.

My first glimpse of a strong emotion from her was in the car. We passed a McDonalds and there was a homeless woman sitting on the curb. Leah said, "I know her. She was at the shelter. Her name is Nia, and she talks to herself. That's her bag with the pineapple on it. She always has it. She is alone too."

Her eyes filled, and her lip quivered. She reached for my change cup and said, "Can we give her this?" We spun around, and Leah jumped out and walked up to her. She put the money on the curb, said nothing and walked away. When she got back in the car she said, "Why do I stay with you now?"

My mind went blank. I had been waiting for her to ask me, and now I was just blank. I said, "Let's get some pie." We pulled into a diner and once the pie came, I talked slowly. "It's a good thing to stay somewhere that is safe. I mean a home, not that you have not been safe. I think…"

Leah looked at me with those shattered glass eyes and sighed, "Aunt Sharon, do you want me to stay?"

"Yes, oh yes!! Carl and I want you to stay. Oh yes, Leah."

"Do you want Lou Ann to stay?"

I had promised myself I would be honest, and Leah's face said she needed to know the truth.

"She can stay as long as she wants. But we both know that won't last."

Leah said, "She needs me." I felt the possibility of Leah running, and panic rose up in my throat.

"Leah, she will be fine. She will come back every time."

Leah took a huge bite of pie and said, with her mouth full, "She will die."

Chapter 14

Lou Ann

Night time. I stood on a corner by one of the fishermen's bars, but the owner told me to leave. "Jesus, give Carl a break, would ya?" I walked down to the bus stop and found a customer. Quick $20, didn't even want to look at me. His car smelled like garbage, and he had wiry black pubic hair. Sometimes I named them; he was Monkey Man.

Mostly that first night I just walked and smoked. Things were jumbled up in my mind. I forgot for a while what town I was in, then I remembered: "Shit Hole City, Oregon." They were all the same to me.

I made it back to Carl's by 6:00 a.m. He was on the back step drinking coffee. "Lou Ann, we need some info on Leah. When did you have her? Where? Did you go to a hospital? All that stuff."

I started laughing and kicking off my high heels. "I found her, Carl." I could feel his eyes on me. "I found her on a splintered floor with no diaper. She had nothing, no one but me and now you."

"Goddammit. Goddammit, fuck, you fucking bitch…" He got up and slammed the door behind him. I heard him whispering to Sharon, and then he left. It felt just like it always did when he left my life, like the air was sucked out of my lungs, like my heart was wide open with no way to fill the hole. Why did I always push him away? I wanted to scream, "I fucking love you!" but I could not do that now. It was too late.

Sharon stepped out and sat down beside me. "Give me a cigarette, Lou Ann." I had never seen Sharon smoke before, but she lit up and sighed like a true smoker. "Lou Ann, has she ever been in a hospital?"

"Nope. She has been healthy."

"How old is she?"

"Maybe ten or twelve. I don't know. No one ever came looking for her. She was just a stray, like me."

"Does she know that?"

I looked at Sharon as hard as I could and growled, "No," but I knew the kid wasn't stupid, so I was lying.

"We have to do some things for her, but it is tricky. They will take her away if we don't do it right. But we'll handle it, the best way, the right way. She won't end up somewhere else."

I couldn't look at Sharon at that moment. I wasn't ready for this yet. It's what I wanted, what I knew had to happen, but I couldn't see it. It was all broken and jagged, no sense to it.

I knew I was not well, but I didn't know what all was wrong with me. There were memories that were clear, but sometimes I was not sure if they were real. My head hurt. I thought all the blows to it had probably caught up with me.

Leah was about two, and she was sitting by the door in the flophouse. She had on no diaper or panties, but she had an empty bottle. She was tiny for two, so maybe she was younger, I don't know.

No one ever came looking for her, and if they had, I would have already moved on. I stole diapers and formula and she slept beside me. She could be left alone. She didn't cry, but she whimpered in her sleep. I wanted her, and she needed someone. I named her Leah. She didn't call me anything at first and then she called me Lou Ann. It worked.

Being her mother was not a talent I had, but I did my best. It was not enough. My work was mostly at night. I didn't make much. We moved constantly. I wasn't proud of it, but I wasn't ashamed either. I knew she was tough, and I knew her mom had to have been a junkie. All that shit is in her. When it comes out, she will need to be able to handle it.

Her earliest memories are with her somewhere deep down…like dark and pooling blood. Somewhere her bare bottom on splintered floors and no food is waiting to burst on the scene. She will need to be tough. Can Carl and Sharon handle it? Will they know how to help her? I just had to be sure.

Chapter 15

Sharon

I am part African American, maybe one half. I knew my mother. She was one of five sisters, and I grew up in their house with kids and chaos. None of them married. Their parents were Norwegians, and they kept the girls close, together, safe, or so they imagined. I think they must have been a little bit kooky or maybe just being strangers in a strange land did it. Anyway, they succeeded at keeping everyone together.

My grandparents were long gone when I was born. My mother, Ana, was the youngest. She was a bit crazy. Maybe it was schizophrenia, I don't know. Aunt Nora was the caretaker of babies and most of the fifteen children who lived in the house off and on. She was the oldest, never worked or had a man. She cooked, sewed, soothed, but she was truly Norwegian stoic; unnecessary emotion was frowned on.

Three of the sisters, Emma, Gudrun, and Ana, learned to work at the fish canneries. They drank whiskey and beer on the weekends and played cards. They all had babies, all colors, and no fathers present.

Aunt Elin had a job as a teacher in Cannon Beach. She came home on Friday nights and left early Monday morning. She was quiet and slim, and she never had children, the same as Nora.

I saw my father once. He came to see me, and Aunt Nora told him I was dead. I had been told to hide upstairs. I watched him leave. He was dark and stocky, and when he walked, I knew he was a fisherman. I wanted to go after him, but I was afraid. Who wants a Norwegian nigger anyway?

I told my mother he came. She was unpredictable, but I did it anyway. I wanted to see what she said. She said, "Oh, I don't know that man."

I had fantasized that I had someone (a father) waiting for me. I had held out hope for something, but it was unnamed. I guess it was that black man who thought I was dead. That was the end of that.

As much as the Norwegians were full of contradiction, they made me who I am, and I like it. I don't know what I got from the man but kinky hair. The Nordheim sisters were my anchor. When I finally left there, Ana was dead, Aunt Nora was blind, and the other cousins and kids had settled into the Nordheim life or left. I saw an escape and I took it. I hitchhiked to Lincoln City and told the bar owner I knew all about mixing drinks. All I knew was a boilermaker, but that was what most of the fishermen ordered. I fit in.

Chapter 16

Leah

Lou Ann started leaving all the time. She came back, but she left again every night. She slept in our bed in the daytime and when I crawled in bed, I smelled her cigarettes, her hairspray, and lipstick.

I tried to mimic our old life, thinking she would stay. I didn't disturb her sleep. I didn't try to get her to eat. I respected her independence, just as she had taught me.

Her clothes were wearing out. For the first time, I approached Aunt Sharon and said, "My mother needs clothes." I rarely used the term "mother," but this felt like a good time to say it. Sharon took me to Value Village and let me select three outfits for

Lou Ann. I knew what she would wear. Then we went to Target and got her underwear and a bra (red and lacey, her way).

When we got home, I quietly took off tags and folded them and put them in her drawers. She didn't really notice. She had no connections to those kinds of things. I saw her wear them, and I felt good. That was it.

Lou Ann was less talkative with me then. She talked with Carl the most. Sometimes the conversation (always out of my earshot) was tense; sometimes they laughed. They had some kind of history, some connection, more than brother and sister. It seemed complex. I left it alone. I was doing what Lou Ann taught me. No questions.

Aunt Sharon showed me two pictures. One was a boy and girl, about ten. They had their arms around each other. They had on shorts and sneakers, and they were scrubbed clean. The back of the picture said 1968, Granny Parsons, 4th of July. It was Carl and Lou Ann. She was skinny in braids. He was a block of a kid with a shock of black hair. They looked like best friends, best pals. I asked if I could have it. Sharon found an old frame. Even though the picture was too small, we put blue paper behind it and I found a starfish sticker to decorate it. It looked great.

The other picture was of an Indian woman. She was small, and her hair was in a long black braid thrown over her shoulder. She was smiling, and her feet were bare. She was standing on the beach and she held a piece of driftwood, like a walking stick. I looked at the back and it said, May Moses, 1960. I asked Aunt Sharon who she was, and she said

Carl's mother. I didn't ask if it was Lou Ann's mother too. I was smarter than that.

Chapter 17

Sharon

Lou Ann was only a ghost before I met her. She was a rarely mentioned lost sister. She was a childhood memory of Carl's that left a flicker of pain in his eyes. Then she was there, in my house. Her looks were a substantial part of her presence. Her hair sparkled. I never liked red hair, but Lou Ann's hair was like autumn: red and gold. The gold glistened in perfect wisps among the auburn strands. Her skin was translucent like only redheads' skin can be, and her eyes were truly the color of the ocean when it reaches its perfect shade of turquoise blue. She had a figure that was beautiful, but she did not feed it. If she had, her beauty would have been devastating.

The bruises, the bones healed without being set, they were there, but they did not detract. Carl was fixated on her. She had control of his emotions, and she was reckless with that power. His eyes followed her from room to room. She was the center for him whenever she was with him.

My kinky brown hair, pulled into a bun, my freckled mocha skin and dark eyes, my sturdy build and short legs – it felt like I was earth and she was sky. I had never been a jealous woman, but all plain women wonder what the power of beauty could do for them.

I focused on the child. The woman, the man, their past and present, I just had to let it go. My heart was in a knot those six months, but they did not know or care.

Carl was just a man. My expectations of men were never high. Maybe it is where I grew up, in a house of women. Men did not have much of a role there. Babymakers.

Carl had always been good to me. No cheating, hardworking, kind, sexy…but a part of him always was missing. When Lou Ann came, I saw the missing piece fill in. It was devastating to watch. His temperament changed. He became edgy, watchful, and a fire I had not seen before was there. It was the dark passion. You could go a whole lifetime and never see that in someone. It is frightening how quickly it consumed him. His face changed. His eyes were deeper brown, and he stared into his own abyss in a way I had not seen before. I was cut off.

If not for Leah, I might have left him there with Lou Ann. Their world was impenetrable. Their conversations were either low talk, their heads tilted intimately toward each other, or shouting matches with Carl getting up, slamming doors or driving away.

Carl and I had never had a fight like that, a passionate fight. We argued, but it was always short and about everyday things. Their fights were loud and angry and full of sparks. She didn't like his agonizing focus on why she had stayed disconnected and why she had this child in tow. She wanted him to forget the why and stay in the present.

Lou Ann's talent for the present was beyond what I had ever seen, even in my own schizophrenic mother. She had no connections to the everyday life, the trappings of a life of cleaning and cooking and eating. She lived in the moment, but as if those moments could be ripped away from her forever.

She wanted life at the fullest – hard and painful, fleeting joy, no plan for comfort. Live hard; it could have been her motto for all I know.

Getting to know her was not for me. I did not want her secrets. Information about Leah did not exist. Nothing to share. She found her and kept her. End of the story. I was angry with that selfishness. It didn't mean I couldn't help Leah. Leah will have her story; Lou Ann cannot rob her of it. At least that is what I thought then. The long-term effects of that blank slate were unknown to me then.

One night I woke up to hear murmurs in the kitchen. It was Lou Ann and Carl. I sat on the stairs and listened. The conversation went something like this:

C. How can you say you have forgotten our parents?

L. Well, I remember them. I just don't care about them. They weren't my parents, for fuck's sake.

C. May tried.

L. Oh come on, she was a ghost in my life. She was a spooky little woman, and she didn't even try to figure me out. She was a goddamn squaw.

C. Jesus, Lou Ann. You were fed; you were clean –

L. I was her husband's toy.

C. She couldn't stop him.

L. So she said.

C. Is that why you live like, like…

L. A whore? No, it's easy work. I'm free, I move around, no ties.

C. Leah is a tie right around your neck.

L. (Laughter) No, she's a companion. My work is lonely.

C. You are fucking sick, Lou Ann. How can you say that? She is a kid.

L. You don't know me.

C. Yeah, well, fuck you, Lou Ann.

L. Well, right back at ya, brother.

I had some questions myself, but I knew the answers well enough. I didn't need her to tell me. I was pretty certain I knew what made her tick. Lou Ann wanted control. She controlled men. She let them hit her, but she called the shots. She controlled where she did her work and when. (Leah told me sometimes they had enough cash to stay holed up for weeks.) She controlled Leah. No one else had any say; she owned her. She was her doll, her childhood. She did not see the tangled hair, dirty fingernails and shabby clothes. She saw her as a child free and protected. She didn't know her own origins, and she had made it. Leah could make it. That was how Lou Ann saw it. The loss of connection was something she stopped feeling when she was a very little girl. She didn't think Leah needed to be connected either.

Chapter 18

Carl

Our father – or rather my father – was named Earl Moses. I don't really know much about him. That was how he and May did things. No information from either of them. I did know he was from Alaska, but I had no idea how he came to Oregon or anything about his family. He was hard as steel and mean like a pit bull. I do not understand how he found May, but somehow, they made me. I am certain I am the best they could do. I know there are people they came from. They must have had some good in them.

Sharon helped me see that good. She saw me as a whole person. She loved me no matter where I came from. Frankly, she didn't really care.

Lou Ann was given to us by a young woman. I was four years old, and I saw the woman/girl in May's kitchen many times. She was so beautiful when I first saw her. She worked at the small grocery in our town. She was all blue eyes and red hair. She laughed a lot and she was fast at her job. I watched her with awe. She was so different than the people around us. They were dark, sometimes drunk, always angry. Times were always tough, and there was not much to be happy about.

One day she brought a little girl to our house. She was skinny with light blue eyes, like a sunny day on the ocean. My mother said, "This is Lou Ann." I took her outside to play, and we never even saw the young woman leave. Lou Ann stayed. It just seemed like it was supposed to happen.

May told us the woman had a problem with drugs and she had to leave because she was dying. We felt sad, and Lou Ann cried, but we were little kids, and each day it got farther away. She was just a memory. Once Lou Ann said to me, "It's okay my mother is dead. I never really lived with her. She didn't love me enough." That was all Lou Ann ever said about her. That is what she believed her whole life.

We played together like there was no tomorrow. I taught her everything I knew. We ran, we climbed, we went to school. I protected her from bullies and soon she was the most popular kindergarten girl.

At that time, Earl was in Alaska for several years, and life was good. May drank but not to the point of passing out. Lou Ann and I shared a room and we had clothes, food, and freedom.

Sometimes May took us to visit Loretta Parsons (Granny). We played with her grandkids and ate big meals around her table. Her husband was crippled, and he sat in a wheelchair smoking a pipe. He had been to war, and we were in awe of him. Looking back, I realize he was an Indian like May. He called May Running Bird and spoke to her in grunts and sounds that she understood. When I asked to speak that way, she acted like she couldn't hear me.

Then Earl came home. Everything changed. It was a game of survival. Little Lou Ann learned fast. She ran fast, ducked fast, and laid low. Sometimes she started fights with Earl, but when she saw May crawl away from him, she stopped that. I do not know how we survived living in Earl's world. Our only blessing was his long trips to work in Alaska.

Chapter 19

Sharon

Carla's mother wanted to know why Leah wasn't registered for school. It was September and she had been at our house since May. I told her Leah was home-schooled, and she frowned. She needs testing, she said. I said she reads better than Carla. She backed off for a while.

How could I get her to school? So many obstacles… I just needed to keep her close by for now. I bought her math books and she completed them quickly. I didn't know her exact age; I just guessed. I bought her harder books to read, and she did read them. I was lost about what to do next. She could do it all. I started to feel better.

Lou Ann started something new. She brought home Pepsi and candy and put them under their bed. I would find Leah curled up gorging on warm soda and candy. Lou Ann brought home ill-fitting and used clothes for Leah, and Leah would come to breakfast in long dresses with scarves for belts. Lou Ann drank beer, but never to drunkenness. Now she brought home cases and drank it warm, sitting on the floor of their room. Leah lined the cans up under the bed.

One morning I found Lou Ann lying across the bed in a black bra and panties. Leah was lying beside her, awake, smelling her hair. They had moved into a world of their own. Leah became very still. Sometimes she just sat at the kitchen table in silence. Sometimes she sat in front of the bedroom door like a guard for Lou Ann.

I asked Carl what he wanted me to do. He said, "Wait. It will soon be over." I waited. It was over right around Thanksgiving.

Chapter 20

Carl

Sheriff Thomas was calm. "How long has she been gone?"

"Over a week."

"How long does she usually stay gone?"

"A night, maybe two."

"Who has she been spending time with?"

"Fuck, Tom, I have no idea! But something is wrong. She's been coming back every night."

"Carl, how long was she gone before now?"

I grabbed my head in my hands. "Damnit. Years, Tom, fucking years."

Tom looked at me and lit a cigarette. "We'll start lookin', Carl, but I cannot put a man on it. Just letting the word get out is best at this point. Let's see what turns up."

As I left, I felt sick. It was guilt, relief, anxiety, all rolled into one. What if we never know? Just like all the shit before us. Fuck it. And what if she crawls in now with no teeth and a busted-up face? How much more can that kid take? How much more can I take?

I went to work, but I couldn't get her out of my mind. The images were horrible, and I thought I couldn't hold up. I played sick and drove to the local fishermen's bar. I drank Pepsi all afternoon. I watched the lowlifes and the drunks. I tried to focus. I was in a silent rage. Fucking Lou Ann.

When I went home, I talked to Sharon about making a plan. She held my hand and agreed. She said, "We're on our own, but we won't let it stop us." I kissed her on her mocha cheek and went to bed.

Chapter 21

Lou Ann

Sometimes I remember the time before Carl, May and Earl. I just see still pictures, like photos. There was a woman with red hair, a girl really. She was standing by a bed with her hand on my forehead, frowning. There is a porch and a little chair. I fit in it, and I have a book about bunnies. Could I read it? I think I could.

No fear is in the pictures. I feel safe. I have not experienced pain yet. There was a table with big people, and I could not see the top. I sat underneath. The legs were all men. Even glimpses of leg hair showed red. I was in a red-headed world.

The time I stayed at May's was like a visit, I thought. There was Carl. I loved him almost immediately. He was so much fun. Rough and tumble, sweet and shy, and he could eat so much. May put six pancakes in front of him. He dug in. I picked at my lone pancake and watched him fold one in half and shove it in. He was showing off.

It was a good time. I missed the redhead, but she was sick when she left me there. She was crying, and I wanted her to go because I wanted to start playing. If I knew it was forever, I would have cried and begged her to take me. I wondered later if she loved me. I thought maybe, but not enough to keep me. I loved Leah more. I kept her as long as I could.

I liked May, but not like I loved Carl. She was not mean. She was always there for us at first. She had a garden, and we had fish drying on racks. Her house wasn't very clean, but it was a home. She had names for us: Carl was Boy Bear and I was Little Wave. Those were our names in her house. I told you that already, I think. That is how my mind is working…not well. She braided my hair every morning, and she made Carl brush his thick flop of hair before we could go out on our adventures.

Right now, I see all this. Tomorrow it might be gone, and all I will remember is a trailer in Seaside. Details line up, then they scramble. People seem familiar, then they are strangers. Men say my name, but I don't know theirs. Sometimes I see a red-headed man and I won't go with him. It's not because I am afraid, but he might be my uncle or my brother or my father.

Then I think of Earl. I pretended he was my father at first. But I soon grew to think of him as a devil man. Sometimes when Carl says something about

Earl, I remember he was a native Alaskan – no red hair. Sometimes I cannot remember him anything but my father. Always, always, always, I remember him as cruel.

Chapter 22

Leah

"Aunt Sharon, she goes to bars. Go to the bars and ask. Oh, and she rides buses. We always rode buses when we had the money." I was pacing on the porch. A week was too long. She couldn't get back to me or she would have. A week was too long.

Sharon changed the sheets, even though I begged her not to. She left Lou Ann's pillow case on the pillow for me. There was a stain of red lipstick on it.

Sharon and I drove from town to town. We put up fliers, but the picture was so grainy. I don't even know where it came from.

People said they saw her. Clerks, bartenders, bus drivers. Some saw her years ago, some more recently. This lady at a bar in Astoria saw her a month ago. She said she ordered two beers, drank them slowly and minded her own business. She said, "I can't forget that hair. It was so pretty." Apparently, she left alone.

All the places were so familiar. I even saw some of our sheds, apartments, hovels, trailers, etc. One that I knew was abandoned (Lou Ann called it "Mouse Shit City") was in Newport. I showed Sharon how to get there. We found stubbed-out Camels, her favorite beer cans and a cheap pair of earrings. She had been there, but Sharon couldn't get the sheriff to check it out. We were on our own.

I heard Sharon and Carl talking one morning. Sharon said, "Thomas just laughed at me, Carl. He said a whore dies every day. He can't keep up with finding all of them." Fucker.

Carl was quiet, then he sighed, and I heard the coffee being poured. "She might have killed herself, you know."

"She's been killing herself. Carl, the pain has to come from a man. It's her addiction. She has to find someone who can do that. She cannot do it herself."

I lay there and realized we might never find her. She could have gone to Portland or even up North. She dragged me all over Oregon and Washington, but we always stayed on the coast, except for our one trip to Portland. Once we lived in a basement of an old house in Gold Beach. I loved it there. The lady upstairs had a cat named Bonnie Blue, and it would sneak into our room and curl up on a chair.

I'm not sure how we stayed there or what Lou Ann was doing. She came home at sunrise every day. She was sweaty, and she had money. She was working at something. She was unhappy, I could tell. But I would have liked to stay there. The beach was wide, and the bridge over the river was pretty. I saw a black bear on the beach one day. Lou Ann said, "Stop lying, Leah." I found a $20 bill there once. I gave it to Lou Ann. At first, she gave me a long hard look and turned me in circles. Then she laughed, and we went to a diner for pancakes and pie.

Carl wouldn't do what Sharon and I did to look for her. He worked, but he didn't want to go where she went. One night at supper he yelled at Sharon. I had never heard him yell. He said, "Every guy has fists, Sharon. You cannot ask every guy if he uses them on women!" Sharon did not respond and kept eating her dinner.

I was sure Lou Ann wanted to survive. She wasn't so old that she would want to die. I just knew she had either gone farther or was hiding. Sometimes we hid for a long time. Especially when she got hurt pretty bad. Then she wanted to heal and rest.

I decided to tell Sharon about her injuries. She asked me if Lou Ann went to hospitals. I didn't know. If she did, I didn't go with her. But she did return with the wired jaw. She sipped beer and milk while I ate pizza. Once her arm was in a sling. Sometimes there were stiches. She must have gone somewhere. Sharon said hospitals would be on our list.

Chapter 23

Sharon

I wanted to stop, but I was driven. I told myself it is Carl, it is Leah, but it was not just them. It was me. I just had to know what happened to Lou Ann. And if she was gone, I wanted Leah and Carl to move away from their obsessions with a wasted woman, one cruel in her own way, fierce and crazy. I wanted them to be free, but more than anything, I wanted them just for me. Selfish, but I thought it could happen. I did not understand then how she would always have them in her grip.

When my mother Ana died in a car wreck, it was two weeks until we knew what happened. She was in a car with Oscar Olson, and they had gone up a logging road for some reason. They were both drunk and when they got together, there was always trouble.

Slippery wet logging roads killed a lot of people. It took a long time for a logger to spot an old blue '54 Chevy's tail gate sticking out of a fern and cedar gully. When they found them, it was Aunt Elin who identified Ana's body. If something needed a professional assessment, they all turned to Aunt Elin.

When they told me, I hid in the shed and cried myself sick. I was twelve years old. Ana was who I slept with each night. She was the only one who knew how to fix my kinky hair. She had two other kids that were older than me, and they had pale skin and blue eyes. They slept in a bed in our room; Lena and Lyle. They were twins. Their grandfather came to see them and sometimes they were gone for a week or more. I liked them, and they weren't mean to me.

Aunt Gudrun had six little kids, all Indians. They were a clan within a clan. They called me "nigger" and yanked my hair. I fought back but there were six of them.

Aunt Nora said they were all from two brothers who worked at the cannery. She said no one could sort out who belonged to whom. They did not visit their fathers. They were always home, and when we walked to school, the blue-eyed twins let me walk between them to protect me.

At school most of us did very well. Aunt Nora made us know things before we were sent off to school. And Aunt Elin, the school teacher, tested us often. I could read very early, and I knew all my numbers. I learned math when Aunt Nora taught me to cook. Nora and Elin were good women.

Aunt Emma had two children by Karl Hansen. He loved her. He begged her to live with him. She would not leave the family. He came often and ate dinner with us. He held Emma's hand and sat Leif and Sven on his knees. I liked Karl very much. He had a heavy Norwegian accent, and he told jokes and stories. He brought candy for everyone. He was the best man we knew.

The other four children were all foundlings, as Aunt Nora said. I'm not sure who found them, but they showed up one by one and stayed. The house was big and rambling. The grandparents had added on as the family grew, and the additions were as crazy and mixed up as the family that lived in them. It was one of the best houses I have ever been inside. It was a bit magical, and it felt old world. There were twists and turns and plenty of rooms. If a closet was needed, one of the aunts built one. They tore out walls when they added more children to their brood. They painted over the boards and called it good. No one ever thought about someone coming in and building. That would have been unnecessary. They could take care of it themselves. They were the women of the house, and they would manage all aspects of the care of the house and the care of the children.

My mother's illness was a worry, and sometimes I heard them discuss it. It was the unpredictable nature of it that disturbed them. Ana was attached to home, but she tended to lose track of things, like where she was and who she was with. Ana was very pretty and had delicate features. She was childlike, and I always related to her like a sister. She loved to laugh and play tricks on her sisters.

Then, when the dark periods of her illness set in, she would curl up in a ball and cry and rock.

Besides fixing my hair and cuddling me in my sleep, she was really only my mother by biology. Her capacity to be responsible was severely diminished. She had the luxury of her older siblings, and they always took up the cause of the children in the household, and that included her. She was my big sister. I loved her, but I could not count on her. I knew that from a young age.

Ana told me and the other children elaborate stories. She had a big imagination and it was populated with trolls and fairies and monsters from the deep woods. I remember Aunt Nora coming into our part of the house and scolding Ana for keeping us up with her story telling. When Aunt Nora closed the door, Ana would put her finger to her lips and motion for us to be quiet. Once we heard the door at the bottom of the stairs close, she would start back with the stories, turning our little bedside lamp on low. That was when I felt closest to her. It was a rich connection, her stories sinking deep into my dreams. But now...what can a grown woman do with trolls and fairies?

In our room was myself, Ana and the twins, Lyle and Lena. It was the only place we existed as a separate "family." Lyle and Lena had their outside life with their father's family. Ana had her job and her many boyfriends. As for me, I had them in our room and the greater world of the Nordheim clan.

I lost touch with Lyle and Lena after I left home. They were absorbed into their father's family and moved to the East Coast when they were teenagers. I could have tried harder to stay connected, but then, they could have done the same with me. I think the connection we had through Ana was strong but hard to name. She was not a grounding element in our life. She was from another place, one we could touch in childhood but then got farther and farther away from.

For all that I ever think about Ana, I do not have hard feelings toward her. She was the best that she could be. Mental illness was not greatly understood by our family, and she never had treatment or medicine that might have made it more bearable for her. When she had a dark period, she tried to stay away from us, and the aunts filled in for her. And she worked, which was of great help to all of the household. Her health caused some absences, but I remember her rising early every morning without complaint. In her own way she carried the stoicism of her family. She loved us, and she never sought to make us unhappy.

I can still smell her sleeping beside me. She had a wonderful scent of baby powder and roses. She kept herself clean and tidy at all times and I remember the feel of her soft hands as we fell asleep. She always stroked my arm as I drifted off. I missed her terribly when she died. I try to imagine now what would have become of her. She probably would have stayed with her sisters, even if I begged her to come and spend her old age with me. The ties to her family were like a sticky web that she could not break free of and of course, when her state of mind was considered, it is no wonder.

My good fortune truly was Nora and Elin. When I left, I sent them letters for a long time. I even visited once, but it was too sad. Nora didn't know who I was; Ana was dead; Gudrun was crippled, and Emma and Elin were very old. Some of the kids were close by. I felt my Norwegian soul there, but my African soul felt lonely.

The aunts were all dead by the time Leah came to us. She was mine and I was hers.

I just needed to find Lou Ann.

Chapter 24

Carl

When May was dying, there was only me to watch her slip away. She died from drinking. It was a pretty long death. I brought her a half-gallon of whiskey every other day that last year. She couldn't eat anymore, and she lay in an old recliner. She drank the whiskey in a coffee cup and she started smoking an old pipe that was in her drawer. She said simply, "It was my father's." Typical May; no information beyond the bare minimum.

She never talked much in the whole time I knew her. She never went to a doctor or a dentist. Lou Ann and I were sent, but May refused.

Granny Parsons had died several years earlier. She had a massive stroke and died on the kitchen floor with a bowl of bread dough tipped onto her chest. She would have loved that. She also would have helped me with May if she had been there.

May wanted whiskey, pipe tobacco and a sketchbook and a pen. She slept, smoked, drank, and drew pictures. The pictures were of birds, tree branches, shells. They were unique, and she could draw long enough that she filled three sketchbooks. Then her hands shook too much. I started finding burn holes in her shifts. I bought her Depends, but she refused them.

The last week I hated to leave, but I had to work. Every day I thought I would find her dead. Then one day she was dead. The whiskey was gone, the pipe was still smoking, and she was slumped forward. I sat with her awhile. I cried another day.

We had never gone to church, and when May meditated or prayed or whatever it was she did, it was a soft swaying in a cross-legged position at the stream out back or at the ocean. When she was in that position you did not bother her.

I closed my eyes and tried to imagine where she might be. I don't have an imagination, so I thought about something I saw her do many times. She sat at the beach, cross-legged, smoking a pipe, sipping a little whiskey and smiling her toothless grin. I decided that is where she would go if she could go anywhere. I had her cremated, and I went to the stream out back and sent her down to the ocean to rest, hopefully in peace.

Then I packed up a few things. I called our landlord and told him I was leaving. I left everything but her pipe, a couple pictures of Lou Ann and me, the sketchbooks of drawings and my clothes.

I didn't know what to do with the belt he beat her with… Finally, I took it up to the old outhouse at the back of our shed. I threw it down the hole. That felt pretty good.

Chapter 25

Leah

When I saw Jenna, I screamed for Aunt Sharon to stop the car. We were in Depot Bay. I jumped out and yelled "Jenna!" She turned, and I knew she didn't recognize me. "It is me, Lou Ann's girl."

Jenna looked better than when I last saw her. That was a few years ago in Seaside. She was working at the 7-11 by day and drinking hard at night. Lou Ann didn't let many people into our world, but she let Jenna stay for a couple of days. Jenna was pretty strung out, and somebody was after her. Jenna and Lou Ann didn't really talk about it. Jenna slept on a folding chaise lounge we put blankets on. She slept a lot. I looked her over while she slept. She was really young; her hair was dark brown and cut about a half inch all over her head. She had a mermaid tattoo on one arm and two nose rings. She had a cross tattoo on her left calf. She was not too pretty but cute in her own way.

She was skinny, and her clothes were all black. Today she had the same look, but her body was fuller, and I recognized the mermaid. She had a backpack with patches all over it and a pit bull on a chain. "Hey, what the hell, kid? What are you doing?"

My eyes filled up and I knew my voice shook, even though I tried hard to sound tough. "Can't find Lou Ann for three weeks now…"

By then Sharon was standing beside me and shook Jenna's hand. After introductions, we sat down on the rock wall. Jenna had been out of the "coast crawl," as she called it, for a long time now. She and her partner had a house just outside town. They were massage therapists. I could see the muscles in her arms then and the way she held herself, like she was doing just fine.

She said Lou Ann had really helped her out when things were out of hand. She was sorry to hear she was missing. Then she tilted her head and said, "Damn. There is something. Rumors of a guy picking up women, a few coming back terrified, a few disappearing."

Sharon jumped up. "Fucking sheriff! Where?"

"Between Yachats and Gold Beach mostly. You can see a flyer at the Newport general store – missing gal from Yachats and a number to call."

Hugs, handshakes, phone numbers exchanged, and we were headed south to Newport. Sharon was focused and quiet. I was trying not to think.

I had felt for a few days that she was dead. It was just a feeling, but I couldn't see her face in my mind anymore. I saw her back and her hair piled up on her head, but no face. Plus, I thought she was in bed with me one morning. I smelled cigarettes and fresh lipstick. I reached over to touch her, and I felt her lying there beside me. I was half awake, afraid to open my eyes. I felt her for a very short time and then nothing. But I smelled her still. I don't know, but it made me sad and very lonely.

We found the flyers and hung one of ours beside them. One had a picture of a girl with long blonde hair. It said her name was Stacey Andrews, and she was twenty-one years old. There was a phone number to call. The other one read:

ANONYMOUS

I GOT AWAY!

BLACK HAIR, SHOULDER LENGTH, MEDIUM BUILD, LIGHT BLUE TOYOTA TRUCK

DO NOT GET IN! THIS GUY MEANS BUSINESS…

There was no phone number.

Sharon called the number on the blonde's flyer. A woman answered. She agreed to meet us in Yachats at a coffee shop. She said she was Stacey's mom.

When we pulled in, Mrs. Andrews was already there. She had on hiking boots and jeans and she looked pretty young. She shook Sharon's hand and we found a table.

Her story was short. Stacey was in a bad relationship – lots of violence. The sheriff's office was sure the boyfriend did it, but he had been in Alaska when she went missing. So, the guy was cleared, and he had been searching for her too.

Mrs. Andrews said she worked right there in the coffee shop.

Mrs. Andrews' hands were shaking, and if you looked closely you saw the daughter's features. "She has been gone two weeks. It feels like we are on our own."

Again, numbers were exchanged, hugs, tears and a long hard hug for me. She touched my hair and said to Sharon, "Watch this little one. Bad men are born every day."

Sharon peeled out and we were on our way to see "that son of a bitch Sheriff Thomas."

Chapter 26

Lou Ann

I was so tired. My shoes were shot. I dropped them in a dumpster. The November wind and rain were brutal. I had to get a better coat and some shoes. I was not going to return to Carl's place. I would not do that to Leah. I remember how my mother left: no tears, no talk. It is the best way.

I found a tiny room in back of the Gold Beach laundromat. It cost $25 per week. It had a bed, sink, toilet and a tiny fridge. I filled it with beer and milk. The rent was no problem. I made that easily. I had found the tour boat captain's bunkhouse. It was off season and various hard-luck fisherman lodged there. If they were fairly clean, it worked out fine.

I also met a couple of guys who liked it together. They were regulars, and I went to the single guy's place with them at least once a week. They paid well and weren't into anything too crazy. They were young and thought they were up to some wild stuff.

I hitched a ride inland one morning and got some shoes and a heavier coat. I stole a couple of slinky tops at Value Village and two pairs of dangly earrings. I was set for a while.

When I was hitching back, a guy picked me up in a little pickup. He wasn't too big, but really muscular. His hair was black, shoulder-length, and he smoked Camels, like me. We chatted. He was asking a lot of questions – too many. I had him drop me off about six blocks from my place. I walked the opposite direction and through some vacant lots. I didn't see him. When I got to my room, I was shaky. Years on the street and you have instincts. He had something weird and sinister about him, I knew it.

Once before Leah, I dated a guy I felt like that about. He had a good car and he got me a job in a little porn theatre taking tickets. He told me to let my boobs show as much as I could. He pulled my bra down and pushed up my tits, tucked the hair behind my ears, gave me new red lipstick and told me, "Do it right. You are the first thing those jack offs see, so rev 'em up good."

He was always checking on me at work then drove me to his place after work. He watched me shower and told me how he wanted me to wash. He made me use a certain shampoo, and he oversaw my makeup.

I tried to joke around about it. He got quiet and said, "Just do what I tell you." I should have left right away, but the attention and control were something I knew about, like with that fucker Earl. I barely got away from that guy alive, just like Earl. These sons of bitches take a piece out of you, for sure.

When I was thirteen years old, I had the latest clothes. I had good makeup, and I got to go to the beauty shop for haircuts. My stupid school friends were in awe. They had no idea the price I was paying.

The regular time was 6:00. May was passed out for the night. Carl was at some sport practice. I knew the routine. Skimpy undies, red bra, slinky dress, red lipstick, hair down. Undress, take it, spanked and into the bathroom. I tried to imagine he was someone I liked, like maybe John Lennon. I told myself the worst was the name calling (you're just a stray dog, a good-for-nothing stray). The act itself was simple but brutal.

When I was about fifteen years old, the brutality came into play more often. He hit me where the marks would be hidden from view: stomach punches, arm twists, real butt bruises. One day after school, when he had left, I talked to May. I had already heard the "I will kill Carl if you tell. I will kill May" talk from Earl, but the beatings were wearing me down. I was forgetting things, and sometimes I had to stay home from school to hide injuries.

May listened as she stood at the kitchen sink. Her back was toward me, that long black braid hanging. She didn't turn around, just pulled a step stool over and got down a box from the cupboard above the kitchen sink and handed it to me. It was full of money. She said in her quiet way, "Go away. Go to Portland. There are places for children. He won't stop, and I cannot make him. He won't stop."

I stared at the money. I thought about how to start, but then I looked at her and said, "No, May. We have to kill him."

May sat down and took a shot of whiskey straight from the bottle. I just cannot remember what happened after that. I blocked it out. I think I killed him. I know I said it before anyone else.

Chapter 27

Sharon

Jesus Christ, there are multiple county sheriffs, but do they talk to each other? My mind was racing, and I was driving like a maniac. Fuck, fuck, fuck…this is ridiculous.

Leah was talking so much all of a sudden. I realized I needed to slow down and listen to her. She was really on a roll. I suggested we stop and sit on the beach and just talk. She was all for it.

I pulled over, and we made our way down a bank and found ourselves some logs to sit on. Leah talked the entire time. Like a stream of consciousness, she rolled out her past for me.

Lou Ann is not my mother, but she likes me to call her that. I don't know my mother, but I kind of remember a room. It's cold and dark and I am afraid. There was no Lou Ann. Lou Ann cannot stop moving. She is really smart. She knows where we need to go every time. Lou Ann loves milk and beer and Camels. Lou Ann never hurt me. She always made sure I was safe. I love her, but she is dead, Aunt Sharon. She is inside of me, like my heartbeat. She has left now, I just know. I can steal anything, Sharon. Do you want me to steal something? Someday I'll find my real mother's family, but I don't know how. I don't even know where they live. Lou Ann can really take a beating. She has been broken up bad. She never complains. Do you think she wants to be hit? How come she never talks about her parents? Is Uncle Carl an Indian? Are you? I'm not afraid of anything. I am very tough. I can do all kinds of things. Lou Ann taught me. Why don't you have some kids? Will you make me your kid? Do you want me to be your kid? I will do whatever it takes. I am really strong, Aunt Sharon. I feel sorry for Mrs. Andrews. I think her daughter is dead. She is a strong lady, but she is gonna suffer. Who is anonymous? I wish we could talk to that person. Lou Ann said possessive men are the worst. I wonder if the guy in the blue pickup is possessive. I know he smokes. The bad ones always smoke.

I was silent. That little woman beside me was an amazing person. She was tough, yet fragile, sweet, but salty – she was all that Lou Ann wanted her to be. She was all Lou Ann's doing. She was marvelous!

After a while she wound down and laid her head on my shoulder. She said, very softly, "Sharon, we can do this. We can find out what happened." I squeezed her close and kissed the top of her head. She was my precious one. My heart was aching with pure love.

Chapter 28

Carl

When I got home that night, they weren't there. The message light was blinking. Sheriff Thomas saying there was information turning up about a couple of missing women – come in when you can.

I sat in the dark kitchen and stared at the stove light. So much of life is just shit. I was tired. I wanted my life back; Sharon, hot food, good lovin', predictability. I didn't want my past in my present. I didn't want those memories haunting me. I was just tired.

If Lou Ann was dead, I was the only one left. Why was I alive? Why was I relatively okay? How come killing Earl didn't make me feel like a murderer?

I really did love May…Running Bird. She was always kind to me, and she tried hard with Lou Ann. But Lou Ann was like a person from another world. May did not know what to do but feed her and tell me to take care of her.

Earl, I never loved. He was a cruel and hard man. He never taught me anything. He always beat my mother. He hurt me every day with what he did to May and Lou Ann.

He treated me the best; a male with his blood, I guess. But I did not love him, and I could not see myself in him. Sure, I was a big man like him. I had his hands and his square shoulders. But I didn't have his black heart. "He was chiseled out of the devil's stony heart." A Granny Parsons' quote after he died.

He spent long months away in Alaska, and if he had been around more, he probably would have died sooner. He drank, but it was not what drove him. He just seemed to feel that all things under his roof were his property. He didn't act like we *owed* him; he just *owned* us. Hard way to come up in the world. I will never know who Earl really was or if he was just a simple mean son of a bitch "carved from the devil's stony heart."

Chapter 29

Leah

I really talked that day. It felt good. Sharon was listening, and she never questioned anything I said. I thought I would do anything to stay with Sharon.

When we got back, Uncle Carl was sitting in the dark. He told us there was a message from Sheriff Thomas. "Good" was all Sharon said. She told me I needed rest, but first a bath. I soaked in the warm bubbly water and thought about the baths in some of our hideouts. Lou Ann called them PTAs (pussy, tits, and armpits).

Sharon laid out clean pajamas. She let me buy everything blue. I noticed my towels were blue now too. A blue heaven...

But sadness and longing for Lou Ann were right there with me. When I was with Lou Ann, life was hard, but it was our own. Whenever someone got too close or too curious or too brutal, we would leave. We were unbound by convention. Time was different. Sometimes days were nights. Sometimes we let others in; mostly we kept them out. Material things were like trash you could throw out. Eating was random and unplanned. Money was for spending, and it didn't matter if you spent it all.

As I soaked in the tub I thought of life without her, here, in this house. I would miss the freedom, but not hunger and dirt. I could live without those forever.

I could not hear Sharon and Carl except for a murmur. I found it very soothing. I slipped into my blue pajamas and crawled into my bed and laid my head on Lou Ann's pillow. I slept like a little baby, saved by Lou Ann. I felt her love everywhere.

Before I woke up I was deep in a dream. There were curtains hanging from the ceiling, and when I walked through one set there was another. I heard the ocean and I thought I was moving toward it. The curtains were heavy, and it took all my strength to push them aside. I was sweating, and my arms were aching. I felt exhausted and I wanted to lie down, but I couldn't. I was closer to the surf, and then the curtain was made of glass, and it shattered when I touched it. Lou Ann was standing there in a black wool coat with a plaid lining. Her hair was wet, and her hands were limp at her sides. I screamed her name and woke up to Uncle Carl hugging me. I gasped and said, "She's in the sea, black coat, plaid lining, in the sea" and then I cried like I was going to die.

Chapter 30

Lou Ann

That fucker was hanging around. I didn't like him. I told my two customers (who like it together) I felt like someone was stalking me. They just laughed and said why wouldn't they; you are hot.

I thought he knew where I was living, so I barricaded my door when I slept. He didn't come close, but I saw him at a distance at some point every day.

Then I met fucking Louis. He wanted me to come to his cabin up the Rogue. He seemed to have enough money, and he really wanted an overnight situation. I was reluctant. It cramped my style. So, I said $250 or it is in your truck. He pulled it out and handed it to me. I should have shoved it back in his face.

The night was going okay, and then Louis asked me if I minded getting roughed up. It made me laugh, and I couldn't stop. Louis thinks he's the first guy who wants it rough? It pissed him off, and he did some serious roughing up. I tried to get him to slow down, but the fists were flying. So, I ran out the door with his keys in my hand and started up his truck. As I peeled out, Louis was running down the driveway naked.

Now what? I had this idiot's truck, my body was aching from punches, one of my teeth was hanging from my gums and my blouse was ripped nearly in half. Fuck, what do I do with this fucker's truck?

When I got back into town, I pulled over at a gas station, dropped the keys on the floorboard and walked back to my place. I knew I had to get out of Gold Beach because Louis would be looking to kill me. I did my usual packing. I left $25 on the table and a note that said, "Thanks. Gotta go."

I had been walking in the dark for a long time, headed north, when two headlights bore down on me. It was the pickup guy. I had no choice but to climb in. My legs were killing me, and I knew Louis would find me if I didn't get out of that town. Besides, this guy intrigued me. What did he want? Why does he give a damn what I am doing? So I got in his truck, and it went to hell from there.

Chapter 31

Sharon

For the first time, we could not soothe Leah. She was beyond comforting. She could not stop crying, and she kept repeating, "black coat, plaid lining, she's in the ocean." She settled some when I wrote it down and showed her. She said that's what we needed to tell people. She was last seen in that coat.

I handed it to Carl and said take it to the sheriff, and he walked out the door. She was still shaky, and her eyes were wild, like the wildling girl we met that first day. I brought a cool rag for her head and gave her some sips of water.

She looked at me, and her voice was so small and sad. "Aunt Sharon, I feel bad that I am so happy here. I feel like I gave up on her. I never want to go back to my old life, but I would if she would still be alive."

I rocked her in my arms and found myself making the same little set of three sighs that Aunt Nora used to soothe me. I even heard myself saying, "there, there little one, there, there." It was helping. She settled down and went back to sleep. As I lay her down, I thanked all the gods in the world for bringing Leah to our doorstep. And, most of all, I thanked Lou Ann.

I left the door ajar as I went down the stairs. I sat down at the table to think. It was only 4:30 a.m. I put on coffee and made a list of what we knew:

- Lou Ann had been gone just over three weeks.
- Another woman was missing.

- There was a description of a suspect from an anonymous person.
- Lou Ann had been seen up and down the coast.
- Leah dreamed she was in a black coat with plaid lining near the ocean.

Leah's information was as legitimate to me as "anonymous." This little wilding girl was in tune with Lou Ann; she had been the only adult in her world. They were like sisters, and they moved in their lives without much more than instinct. If Lou Ann wanted Leah to help us find her, I believe she could do it.

I had always believed in ghosts and spirits. The Norwegian aunts told stories passed down from their parents about fairies, ghosts, and trolls. The Nordheim sisters thought that their mother lived in our house as a spirit. They called her Mama

Magda. If things went missing, Magda did it and for a good reason. She had not believed in excess. If you had a bad dream, they said Mama Magda had chased the bad spirits away. Some of us thought we saw her. A small white shimmer, a footstep in the hall, a whisper. So many times, the refrigerator door would be open when Aunt Nora went down at the first crack of light in the sky to prepare our breakfast. She said Mama Magda never had a refrigerator and she was fascinated. She said the cold reminded her of Norway winters.

Once I thought I felt Magda's hand on my forehead when I was sick with a horrid case of the mumps. I opened my eyes, and it seemed like a shimmering light was all around me. I could feel her small hand. She lingered for a moment and then she was gone. When I told Aunt Nora, she clucked her three-sigh rhythm and said, "She accepts you are her granddaughter – is good!"

So you see, I believed completely that Lou Ann came and showed Leah what she could. Just as I was pouring my coffee, Carl came in and sat down hard. He dropped his head in his hands and sobbed silently.

Chapter 32

Leah

Once Lou Ann left me with a woman in Astoria. It had never happened before. I was probably seven or eight. The lady was someone who seemed to already know Lou Ann. I was told to call her Mrs. Bonham. Lou Ann sat me on her lap and said, "I will be back, promise. Mrs. Bonham just needs to take care of you for two nights. I will come in two days, and then we are going on a bus trip."

I started to whimper, and Lou Ann looked me in the eyes and said, "Tough. Always be tough, Leah."

When the door closed, I looked around Mrs. Bonham's living room. It was full of furniture. There was barely room to walk. The furniture was all old, and there were pillows on everything. She had a big fireplace with a picture of a sea captain above the mantle. It smelled musty, but it also smelled like some kind of spice. Mrs. Bonham was older, and she had on a lavender dress with matching belt and nylons. Her hair was white and permed. She had on earrings that matched everything. She said, "Dear, let's have some sandwiches."

Her kitchen was bigger than any room Lou Ann and I had ever stayed in. It was very clean, and it had a yellow table and chairs and yellow checked curtains. She made us tuna sandwiches with pickles that were delicious. We had glasses of cold milk. Afterward, she cut us slices of chocolate layer cake. I wasn't used to sitting at a table with china plates, real silverware, and glasses that weren't plastic cups from 7-11. It all was so beautiful.

Mrs. Bonham talked about her late husband, Richard. He had been a sea captain. His ship was called the Eleanor, after her. He was out at sea often, but they were very happy. They had only one child, Edward, but he died as a baby.

All this was said before the cake. I asked her how she knew Lou Ann. "Oh, I used to rent a house to her family when she was a little girl." As I started to ask more questions, she stopped answering. She simply said, "It was so long ago, dear."

As she was cleaning up the kitchen it seemed to me she was chatting with someone else, but I could not really tell. It was more like she was murmuring under her breath, and she even giggled a couple of times. But I had not had a lot of exposure to different kinds of people. I thought maybe it was just something old ladies did.

Her house was three stories high. We toured it all. I could not imagine how she could live in such a mansion. She had views of the Pacific Ocean and the Columbia River. It was a wild and beautiful part of the river as it rolled into the Pacific. The waters swirled, and white caps were everywhere. It made my heart pound. The floors were hardwood, and the carpet on the stairs was black with pink roses. Every room was full of furniture. The smell of a musty old house filled my lungs. Mrs. Bonham talked the entire time and just like in the kitchen she seemed to talk to someone that I could not see. I thought she seemed almost like a ghost herself, floating through that house as if I could see right through her. She told me Mr. Bonham had left her a lot of money. She had a housekeeper and the housekeeper also did her shopping. "I still cook, but I don't like to go to the store anymore."

In one huge bedroom, we looked at a closet full of fancy dresses. She said she had had to dress for many dinners held by people her husband did business with. She had so many colors and styles. She laid them on the bed and talked about where she got them, where she wore them. All the time she was talking to someone else in the room. Her conversation wove me in, but she never identified our companion. I was the guest, and the other person/spirit/ghost was always there. Like most of my childhood, I didn't question. It was just the world of adults.

We must have been an interesting pair. Mrs. Bonham tastefully dressed, hair in place, low heels, violet earrings. I was in one of my assorted Value Village outfits, too big, tied on, old sneakers, hair coming out of my braids. Mrs. Bonham kindly did not try to straighten me up. She asked if I wished to bathe before bed. I was too shy to say yes.

I slept in the room across the hallway from hers with both bedroom doors open. She left on a night light for me, but darkness was not one of my fears. I didn't say anything. She left the window open, and I could hear a light rain and wind. I lay there wondering about Lou Ann. I made myself believe she would come back for me.

I woke up in the night and heard Mrs. Bonham whispering to someone. I even heard her laugh. I crept across the hall to see who it was, but there was no one. She was propped up in her bed, talking to no one. I watched her smile and gesture and realized she was being flirty, like Lou Ann would be with her men. It was so weird, totally weird. I slipped back into the bed with the clean sheets and put a pillow over my head.

The next morning Lou Ann turned up while Mrs. Bonham was preparing oatmeal with peaches and wheat toast with strawberry jam. I had just shoved in my second piece of toast when the doorbell rang.

Lou Ann looked pretty rough. Her hair was greasy, and she had it in a top-notch bun. She had a bruise on her cheek and her jeans were dirty. Mrs. Bonham simply pulled out a chair and said, "Have some breakfast, dear." I knew Lou Ann could not eat in the early morning, but she politely took a couple of bites. I could see her gag.

"Did plans fall through, Lou Ann?"

"Yes. We are leaving today. I heard I could get a job at a fish factory in Portland. I can find Leah a school there."

I looked at Lou Ann and she shook her head "no" when Mrs. Bonham turned to get the coffee. We sat for a while longer, and then Lou Ann thanked Mrs. Bonham for her kindness. When we stood to leave,

Mrs. Bonham pressed money into Lou Ann's open hand and kissed her cheek. "Please bring your delightful girl to see me again, dear."

When we walked down her steps, I turned to wave at her. She was standing there chatting with her invisible friend. I knew she was telling them about Lou Ann. I wished I could hear what she was saying.

When we got to the bus depot, Lou Ann asked me if I had met Mr. Bonham. I said, "He's dead." And she chuckled. "Not for Mrs. Bonham. She has been talking to him for years."

That was my first introduction to the world of the dead amongst the living. I could understand that Mr. Bonham was as real as anyone else to Mrs. Bonham. With the understanding that only children can conjure, I felt very sure that there were ghosts among us all.

Chapter 33

Carl

In all my life, I hope I don't have to do anything again like I did that December. Identifying Lou Ann's body was gruesome. She had been in the water for at least ten days; that's what the coroner said anyway. She had a split lip and what he described as multiple body contusions and a serious head wound, in the back, which killed her. Her hair was tangled and fanned out, but it still glinted in that weird light of the morgue. She looked ghostly. All I could say was, "That's her."

The sheriff was talking to me in the upstairs hallway, but I couldn't really hear him. Some kind of pounding was in my head, and I couldn't catch my breath. I was suddenly on the floor, and a paramedic was standing over me. "Carl, Carl, you okay?" It was Leon Gray; I grew up with him. I struggled to stand. "Yeah, just need some air."

Outside it was a cold and rainy morning, but I felt better. Sheriff Thomas asked if I wanted a ride home – no thanks. "There are really no personal effects, Carl." I was not surprised. When he said she was wearing jeans, a ripped blouse and a black coat with a plaid lining, my knees buckled again. I heard the sheriff say, "Leon, drive him home."

When I got there, Sharon let me sob quietly. She poured some coffee and sat until I was ready. She said, "Gone?"

"Yes, I saw her."

I told her what the sheriff was thinking. Some guy knocked her around pretty good. He either pushed her over or she fell in. She went in backward.

Anyway, that was the theory, due to the injuries on the back of her head.

Sharon asked me if I wanted to be the one to tell Leah. I said yes. Then she said, "She knew, Carl."

I nodded my head, and she started to say something, and I said, "Yes, the coat was just like she described."

We just sat there and let it sink in. I saw Lou Ann running and laughing, strawberry hair shining and poking out of her braids. I heard her whispering in our room when we were supposed to be sleeping. The Lou Ann on the slab was not that girl, my childhood love, my childhood companion. But, of course, she was, and that could never be changed.

It was too much, but I had to pull myself together. Leah would be awake in a few hours. There would be things to do and more conversations with the sheriff's office. But right then I was filled with a deep, bone-crunching, blinding guilt. It was so consuming it threated to sink me. The reasons go back to when we were kids.

Lou Ann and I were close, so close. We finished each other's sentences, and I always finished her sandwiches. When Earl was gone, which was often when we were under twelve, we lived a life of freedom. May did not have restrictions, except attending school.

We liked school. We had friends. Lou Ann helped me in math and I helped her in English.

We knew our small towns well. We moved only twice in the time when we were little, and Earl and May rented houses in neighborhoods with kids. We knew Mrs. Bonham in Astoria and Granny Parsons in the town where we spent most of our time.

May wasn't a PTA-type mother, but she insisted on being polite. Lou Ann's hair had to be braided and our clothes were always clean.

Earl's brutal nature was a fact of life. We were good at running. We hated when he hit May, and we begged her to resist. She always said the same thing; he won't stop.

Once May moved us up north for a job when Earl was in Alaska. Mrs. Bonham's guest house in Astoria was better than our old house for sure. The beds were softer, and the kitchen was bigger. May drank in the evening, but not too much. Her days were filled with chores at Mrs. Bonham's.

Lou Ann and I were free to roam the town, but we mostly loved to explore the big house. There was a little brick path from our back door to the gate into Mrs. Bonham's back yard. We entered through the kitchen as May had instructed. We were as quiet as two eight-year-old children could be. Mrs. Bonham kept the cookie jars full, and we could indulge. She baked beautiful cakes and breads. May scrubbed, dusted and shined, but she did not cook. That was the realm of Mrs. Bonham.

Lou Ann liked the very top floor of the house the best. It was once a maid's quarters. It had two half-moon windows with wavy leaded glass and a view of the Columbia River and the Pacific Ocean. It was an open room with slanted ceilings. It had a bed, a dresser, a small table and chairs, an oval rug worn and frayed, and a vent that let in heat from down below. We brought things to play with to the room and spent hours coloring, drawing, talking, building and being children. Safe.

But it was there in the maid's quarters that I would lose Lou Ann. It made her quiet and withdrawn sometimes. She went inside to places I could not go and she had the same look on her face that I remember from when she brought us Leah. Lou Ann could be passionate and focused and angry and wild, but when you tried to respond to her or join the flow of her energy, she was already gone. I have never known anyone who could close you out as completely as Lou Ann. It left you longing.

Lou Ann was never really ours. She belonged to anyone for a moment but no one for very long. Maybe something made her that way, or maybe she just came that way. We never knew. Maybe we were part of it, and our dark eyes and dark hair and quiet acceptance of life was something she wanted to separate herself from. She never told us, but we never really had her. It was always that way with Lou Ann, from the start, even before Earl's abuse.

Love for Lou Ann was not easy. I believe she loved us, but not the way we loved her. It wasn't that she had expectations that were beyond what we could give her. It wasn't that she felt unloved. She had the rare and unnerving gift of being fully in the present. She did not need security, tenderness, safety or commitment. All that she seemed to need was life at a full force: hard and intense and fast. She could light up your world so that the air sparkled, but when she withdrew, it was drab and lonely.

Real problems started when we moved into puberty. We had always shared a room, and we worked around the embarrassments of our changing bodies. I noticed Lou Ann was growing boobs, and I vaguely wondered when she would have to wear a bra. My voice was changing, and my forehead was covered in zits.

She flirted with boys. I flirted with girls. We laughed at each other, got into some fights, locked each other out of the room. Not that any of our rooms had locks. Abusers like Earl are funny about locks. They want to lock you in, but they don't want to be locked out. We learned from May how to barricade doors and windows.

I knew Lou Ann was very pretty. Everyone told her she was. Her hair was a big deal – lots of dark-haired people around her. The red with blonde highlights literally shone in our gray coastal weather.

Lou Ann was not someone who required much in the way of stuff. She never took good care of anything – always losing things. Her clothes were thrown on the floor, her bed unmade, makeup all over the bathroom…

But one day she came home with Earl from Tillamook. She had several shopping bags, and she stormed into our room where I was lying on the bed reading. She shoved the bags under her bed. Then she laid down, curled up in a ball and faced the wall.

I pulled out the bags. She didn't move. There were clothes in her size: fancy panties and bras, slinky slips, hair clips, makeup. There were jeans for school and tops and shoes. I said, "What the fuck? Where did you get this shit?"

She didn't answer. I pulled her by the shoulder; she was quickly wiping away tears. "Leave me alone."

I went downstairs and found May out back. She was doing her thing, cross-legged, swaying, murmuring. I waited until she got up and asked her, "Did you see that stuff Earl bought Lou Ann?"

She looked at me with tear-filled eyes and said, "He won't stop." I yelled at her, "What? Stop what? What is going on here?"

May touched my arm, but as I pulled away, she said, "She is a stray, not his. He does not feel anything for her; it is a bad thing."

At thirteen, trying to sort out this mess was difficult, but I understood it was dangerous and Lou Ann was the one in danger. It was then that May began pushing me into sports. It was a time when I was her only child, and she was saving me.

I hate that I wanted that love from May enough to abandon Lou Ann. I started every activity— track, football, basketball, summer baseball. I was a natural athlete and was swept up in the world of small town sports. I was a local hero, captain of every team I joined.

School, sports, school, sports, stay away from home, even if Earl is gone. School, sports, girls, stay busy all of the time.

Lou Ann became paler, thinner, angrier. She missed school more. I saw bruises. I caught her looking at one on her shoulder in the bathroom mirror. She slammed the door in my face.

I was a fucked-up brother. I just kept practicing everything. I was good at cross-country, and I got to go to Eugene to summer camps. May kept me moving. She was sacrificing Lou Ann to save me. I know that now. I knew it then.

How bad it felt, deep down, I didn't realize until I was fifteen years old.

It was winter, and there was a break of one week between football and basketball seasons. I came into the kitchen. Lou Ann was saying to May, "We have to kill him." May was drinking straight from the whiskey bottle.

I grabbed the bottle and said, "Knock it off, May. Lou Ann, we'll do it." Just that fast I said I would kill my own father. What turns and twists must life take before a boy can state that, simply and with such conviction?

Lou Ann started to tear up, then she sucked back her pain, like only Lou Ann could and said, "Good."

I didn't think about what it meant or the consequences or anything you'd imagine a person would think. It was all about *how* and *when*. The plan took all three of us to carry out. We planned for only two days and then we were ready to execute the plan, execute Earl. May knew how to make him fall asleep. She would not tell us what she was using. She just said, "He will eat his dinner and sleep hard."

I could drive. He was big and heavy. All three of us dragged him to the pickup and pulled him into the front seat. It was pitch-black November, midnight. Lou Ann got in beside him. She brought a hammer, just in case he came to.

I drove without lights until we got to side roads. Then we headed up a steep old logging road. We knew where we were, and we knew Earl went up here often to talk to loggers he knew from Alaska.

Earl was starting to groan as we drove. I pulled over, and we hopped out. We dragged him in front of the steering wheel, put the car in gear, shut the doors and pushed him over the black, wet, wooded cliff.

The rain drizzled, and we listened to the truck crashing against trees. We heard the horn, long and frightening, then nothing. It was too black to see into the canyon. Lou Ann crouched in the ferns and listened for sounds of movement. The hammer never left her hand.

It took us three hours in pitch-black slippery wet Oregon coast weather to make it back home. We were quiet, but Lou Ann did say, "The rain washed out our tracks." Then she said, "Carl, if he makes it out of that canyon, I will kill him with this hammer. He has to sleep sometime." I said, "I know, sis. I will be right there with you."

When we got back May was not drunk. She was sitting in the dark waiting. We came in wet and cold. She made coffee and pancakes. We put our clothes in the washer, put on our pajamas and waited for daylight. That was that…

That is why when she came back to us with Leah, I was consumed with rage toward her. I had lived my childhood in love with my sister, not always feeling like a brother but desiring her like a lover. I had killed my father for her, and then she left me. I can't describe what that was like, when she just gone, gone as if she'd never been with us at all.

I had worked hard to erase her from my life. When I found Sharon, I found the opposite of Lou Ann, and it was good. Then she comes back with all of her life force and brings this innocent child with her. It was all too much to bear, and I agonized about her every day until she died.

There would always be what Earl did to her, to all of us. He robbed us all. He just took her youth and her beauty and used it. He never cared about what it did to any of us. He grabbed, he hurt, he slapped, he punched, and then we made him die.

Without Lou Ann, he would have lived longer. May and I did not have the strength without her. Lou Ann did not worry about what it might do to May or to me. She lived in the present. She reached a day and a time and something inside of her snapped, and it was over. I did all I could physically to help kill him, and I did it in the body and mind of a man. Killing Earl made me a man, just not the one I wanted to be.

Chapter 34

Sharon

When Lou Ann and Leah arrived, I did not have the whole story. Carl had never shared the death of his father or what led up to it.

He recalled his childhood with a boy's eye for the sports, the freedom, the food, the ocean. He said his sister was adopted and she had run off in her teens. I swear he said it was because she was like her mother, a wanderer. He said he never told me that. He said he told me she was always wild. Whatever; she was not just wild. She was caged and treated with disregard, enslaved to the man who ruled their house. A cruel monster. But that story didn't come until she burst into our lives.

Too much came then. The horror of their past filled my peaceful home. The dark energy that was always hanging off of Lou Ann was something I could almost see.

Sometimes I thought I walked through shadows while she was there; dark and heavy energy. I thought I saw it hovering over Leah while she practiced writing at the kitchen table, her head bent in concentration.

The Norwegians believed in spirits, but there was a practical side to their beliefs. If you want the good ones, welcome them. If you want the bad ones to leave, show them the door. Sweep them out, like the dirt on the floor.

So, I set my mind on showing them the door. I brought in many bouquets of flowers, kept things extra clean, painted, baked, open windows. I spoke to them in my mind, fearless words like "You are not staying here in this house of light." I burnt sweet grass and white sage smudges. I sang hymns from my childhood. I fought this battle alone with one goal in mind; do not attach your energy to me and mine, which now included Leah. This is not your home. When Lou Ann disappeared, they went with her. I won.

Chapter 35

Leah

When I woke up, Uncle Carl was sitting on the bed. He was running his hands through his thick black hair. He looked so tired and sad. I knew she was really dead now. All I could say was, "She loved me."

He picked me up and rocked me in his arms and said, "And we loved her. We really loved her."

We stood like that for a while. Then he said, "Let's see if Aunt Sharon will make us some pancakes and coffee."

I accepted the black coffee, and I have never stopped drinking it. It was my first morning as a grownup. I think I was probably twelve and a half.

I think I had been growing up pretty fast ever since I could remember, but that morning was a turning point.

We were quiet but peaceful that morning. It was just the three of us in Aunt Sharon's warm little kitchen. We all loved each other, and we could stop worrying about Lou Ann. I vowed right then that I would never give Carl and Sharon reasons to worry about me if I could help it.

Lou Ann saved me from total neglect. She protected me as long as she could. She was broken in pieces in her head, her heart, but she managed to keep a thread of sanity and attached it to me.

She may have been a stray, a whore, a lost soul, but she knew how to protect me, and she brought me here to a house of love.

Uncle Carl had a necklace made for me in the shape of a silver wave, and he had it engraved on the back; Lou Ann Little Wave. Aunt Sharon had her ashes put in an urn the light blue of her eyes and told me I could do what I wanted to do with it. I left it in the room I shared with her. In summer, Sharon and I picked little bouquets to set beside it: sweet peas from the roadsides, wild daisies, wild lupine, fireweed, wild roses, all the wild beauty we could find.

My schooling continued at home. Carla kept coming over, but I was far ahead of her in all things that required intellect. I had had too much exposure to the world, and she had not had enough. We were a strange pair, but we knew each other, and we kept up our odd connection. I guess Carla didn't have any other friends. I never really thought about that because I wasn't at school with her, but I see it now.

She wasn't the kind of girl who fits in well, though she fit in better than I did.

Sharon worked hard on getting me identification. I took the family name, Moses. I got to pick my own birthday, so I picked December 1st, the day they found Lou Ann. A doctor's exam determined I was thirteen years old, just like I had guessed. I had some cavities, but my teeth were straight.

When people commented on my looks, Uncle Carl said, "She's a lot more than a pretty face." He protected me from all males until I heard Aunt Sharon say, "How will she be able to get along if she doesn't meet a boy or two?"

People thought we were a nice little family, but I'm sure they wondered who I looked like. I had that in common with Lou Ann. I found out that was Sharon's experience too.

Sharon insisted Carl share things about Lou Ann and their life as children. I learned about the red-headed girl, the way Lou Ann was called a stray, the cruel Earl and the incapacitated May. Each time I see redheads I wonder, but there is no way to trace anyone. Carl told me she was a junkie, not from where they lived, and when she left Lou Ann with his mother no one told him anything, nor did they tell Lou Ann. He knew of no family connection between the red-headed woman and May, but for some reason she left Lou Ann with the Moses family. Just another unknown.

I know I will never know my people, who I come from. No one knows the story of how I ended up with Lou Ann. She told Carl I was just left and she thought I was two years old or close to it. I have adjusted to no information. I tell myself I am free to be whatever I want. But deep in my heart, I long to meet someone with my weird eyes and maybe some other feature that would lead me to believe they were my family, and they would know me at first sight. It will never happen. Lou Ann and Leah, little stray women, tough, smart and on their own…that is where I come from.

For a long time, I kept it all as simple as I could, but that was before I let myself dig deeper.

Chapter 36

Lou Ann

When I climbed in that blue pickup, I thought to myself, this would be a good day to die. This guy will probably kill me, maybe quick, better than letting Louis find me.

The guy looked like Earl. So ironic, so fitting, that the guy who killed my innocence, who left me battered and broken, might as well get in that last punch.

He was chatty as usual, asking about my split lip and so I turned to him and said, "People give me money to have sex. Sometimes they aren't too nice." He muttered something like 'stupid bitch' and I pushed him farther. "Oh, you are better, fucker? You pick me up, you stalk me, you creep me out, but you don't pay me? What weird shit is going on in your head?"

He shifted down and made a hard turn down a dirt road. The dark wet leaves, the low fog, I knew it all. I could hear the angry surf coming. He pulled me out of the truck and marched me right up to the cliff. As we walked, I thought of Leah. *She is safe; she is asleep in our bed at Carl's. She can read. She will be smart. She is a stray, but now she purrs like a sweet little blue-eyed kitten.*

He was strong this guy, determined. I anticipated he would push me over the cliff and into the ocean. I was ready to die, and I calculated I could pass out before the pain, but my heart was racing, and I had no air left in my lungs. Wanting death and facing death are different, but if you are seeking suicide through someone else's hand, you have to accept their methods. It is a collaboration. Once he pushed me, it was a long fall, and I left my body behind. I saw myself falling from above. I looked like a skinny drenched whore with a heavy black coat with a plaid lining. I hit the rocks below and then rolled into the water. The waves knocked me against the rocks. Goodbye, Little Wave.

Chapter 37

Sharon

His name was Warren Moses. They got him on two counts of murder, two counts of kidnapping. The damage to Lou Ann's body helped tip the judge toward life in prison. He looked like Earl, anyway that was what Carl said. He said, "The last face she saw was our old man." It bothered him.

I did some research on Carl's ancestry. Since Leah was asking questions, I decided to try to find out more. It was highly possible that Warren was a cousin to Carl. The birth records in the Alaskan Inuit Village where Earl was born were not always accurate. But a relationship was possible; strange but possible. I decided not to pursue the dark recesses of the Moses clan history. Better to leave that shallow end of the gene pool alone.

Leah wanted to visit with Mrs. Andrews, Stacey's mother. We met her at the same place as before. She looked older this time, and her eyes had that strange hollow look that only intense grief can bring. We knew from the trial that Stacey was found in a wooded area not too far from where they found Lou Ann. She had been bludgeoned with a stick of wood. They found Warren Moses' DNA on the stick and his muddy footprints all around her.

We shared stories about Lou Ann and Stacey. We stayed clear of the worst parts of their lives. Both had strong independent natures; both let men hit them; both were young and beautiful. They both were headed toward disaster of some kind. Warren Moses targeted them for death because they were battered. It sickened him; that is what he said on the stand. He said they should have fought back or stopped whatever it was that caused the men to hit them. He said he would have done it again. They were as despicable as the men who hit them. I wanted to kill him with my bare hands.

Leah was doing remarkably well, but we still worried about the consequences of growing up in a world where women were punching bags. Counseling would come, but we tried to give her some space. She asked questions, but they were not often about the past. She was looking forward, like a young woman of thirteen should. Miraculously, she felt peaceful about Lou Ann.

What had Lou Ann taught Leah? Some of it was not good, of course. You cannot romanticize hunger, stealing, accepting and seeking out brutality. You cannot turn your back on the lack of communication with family and keeping her from schools and other children.

What was good? I kept asking myself and the very best summation was the love she felt for an abandoned baby girl and her determination to protect that little stray. That was it. That was the best she had to give, and she poured it into Leah. Like I have said before, thank God Lou Ann brought us Leah, our own Little Wave. Those were my feelings then, but, as the years passed, and Leah began to remember her life with a hooker, I didn't feel much love for Lou Ann. I just wanted to kill her, but she was already dead.

Chapter 38

Carl

Sharon and Leah are at the grocery. The sky is unusually blue today with wispy white clouds. I am off work this week. We talked about taking a little trip, but Sharon and I sense Leah's need for stability.

I repainted Leah's room and she picked blue, just like Lou Ann's eyes – sea blue. I painted the kitchen pale yellow, and Sharon hung new white fluffy curtains. We mowed and edged the yard, tilled the garden and looked forward, just like our Leah.

How lucky are we to have her? She is precious. She is a gift. She is tough like Lou Ann taught her.

I know the ugliness she witnessed is somewhere inside her, but I can only try to help if it comes out to hurt her.

When I brought her the silver wave necklace she told me it was her first piece of jewelry and then she giggled and said it was perfect. I see she wears it every day, along with her blue wardrobe. She lets her hair fall down her back more, but many days she braids it – a little bit of May in our life.

She asked me if she could frame some of May's drawings. We made a collage of them and hung it in the living room. Now that I see them through Leah's eyes, they are more beautiful. All that was hidden in my mother, just like everything in her life. In her own quiet yet powerful way, May saved me from being like Earl, like so many other men around me. She made me work hard, see my own potential, pushed me to be safe. She saved me, but she could not save Lou Ann. Maybe a different woman than my mother could have pulled us out of that deep hole, but she did not. I want to ask her why, but the chance has come and gone. Living with May all those years, I doubt that she would have been able to articulate her reasoning.

After the shock of Lou Ann's return and her death, I started to feel like more of the history of Lou Ann's and my childhood should be shared with Leah. Even Sharon was not fully aware of all of it. She knew it in pieces, but this time I wanted to get the whole thing out. It wasn't just my history that mattered. These two women left in my life, that I loved with all my heart, deserved the whole story.

I can tell you, it was a lifting of a burden for me, but I still wonder if it was selfish timing. I am not sure Leah was ready, but I cannot really go back and change the fact I told her when she was about fourteen years old, right at the age Lou Ann was when these events took place.

The House of Moses

Told to Leah by Carl

The Murder

My father was a cruel man. He never said anything that was kind or caring; at least I never heard it. He was often silent. He ate the food put in front of him, drank the whiskey his wife poured for him, worked every day and was often absent from our lives. But when he was present, it was like living with a volcano: quiet and smoky and then boiling hot and destructive.

He never gave us any indication that he loved any of us. There was no touching, except to whip or slap or punch. He never spoke our names except to scream them. He was a big man and his hands seemed huge to all of us. The grip was hard, and if you were caught, you were not released without physical pain and punishment.

My mother was so quiet already. She seemed like a shadow in the house when he was there. She moved quietly and did all that he wanted, but when he was feeling mean, it didn't matter. Then he used her like a punching bag, for no reason but that she existed. I still don't fully understand why she took so much abuse. She would not talk about it, period. I can imagine so many reasons, but they are all just speculation. She never spoke of it.

When we made the crazy decision to kill Earl, I think she agreed because there were no alternatives. She always told us that he would not stop hurting us. I don't know what she knew about him or if she just knew that men like that cannot change. Either way, she did not argue or try to talk us out of it. She just helped us plan his death. She was a full partner in our triangle of killers, our trio of survivors.

At the time we murdered him, he was working in the woods not far from where we lived. His trade had always been logging and some fishing. To make enough money to make ends meet, he moved from the Oregon coastline to Alaskan interiors and coastlines to find work. He never complained about working. He also never talked about money. He was a simple man in many ways. But he never seemed to have a moment of joy. I don't recall hearing him laugh, seeing him smile, even small talk. Whatever made Earl the way he was must have been brutal, because in my short life of knowing him, he was dark and angry. I have no memories of any other emotion.

May's role was to mix up "something" that would knock him out after supper. She put it in his whiskey. I remember we ate venison stew that night, with buttermilk biscuits. It was silent as usual. When he was gone, Lou Ann and I talked non-stop at the table, but it was best to be quiet around Earl. He might not notice you were there and not reach over and slap your head. So we were eating our stew, and he was sipping his whiskey between huge bites. When he passed out, it was gradual. He walked to his chair, slumped down, yelled for more whiskey and then he went out.

We were cautious at first because you don't want to wake a huge man from sleep, especially when he is Earl. We poked and jumped back, yelled his name, made loud noises, but he didn't move. It took all three of us to carry his dead weight to the truck. We had no neighbors, and so it was not like we had to hide from anyone. We dragged him and lifted him into the seat. It was almost impossible because May and Lou Ann were such tiny women, but they mustered up the strength, and we shoved him in. May had branches and was sweeping away the tracks where we dragged him across the driveway. Then it started to pour rain as we pulled away.

Lou Ann was focused. If he had come to in the truck, she would have clobbered him with that hammer, and of course that would have complicated everything. But luckily, May's drug kept him down long enough for us to carry out the deed.

We were so close to him physically on that ride. I had never been that close to his body ever. Of course, Lou Ann, that was a different story. But for me, his smell, his bulk, his breathing, all of it was making me want to puke. Not because I found him so repulsive, but because I knew he was going to die in a short time and I was going to do it. I was fifteen, not a man, just a boy. I had never had any father but Earl. Try to imagine how this was for me. As much as I hated him, I loved him. As much as he hurt my mother and sister, he never hurt me as much. As much as we needed him to die, I didn't want him to die at my hands. I am not sure how I did it. It has haunted me all of my life. I haven't gotten over it. You just don't get over some things.

Everyone always wants resolution. If only we could resolve this and that. People spend so much time in their life looking for resolution. Earl's death taught me that some things are never resolved. They will never be all right. They will never stop haunting you. They will just become a piece of who you are, and you will have to live with it. We do carry our baggage everywhere we go and the dream of shedding it is a false hope for most of us.

The really big things stay, and so do many of the little things. They are who we are, even if they are ugly. Maybe if we didn't call it baggage, just life, it would be better.

When we got to the best spot in the road, the rain was coming down in sheets. It was so black out you could not see the hand in front of your face. All we had were the dash lights to see by. The mechanics of getting him in place and shoving the truck over the cliff were not too hard. We worried the truck might not go far enough down or that he might not sustain an injury that would kill him. That is why the location was so important. It had to be very steep. It needed to logically be a spot where he could miss a turn, and we had to be able to get out in time. But, as you know, it all worked.

When we were pushing the truck, I glanced over at Lou Ann. I could not see her face, but I could hear her grunting and see the faint outline of her small, childlike frame. I pushed harder, for her. Only for her at that moment. I killed him for her and her alone. I knew it then and I know it now. I loved my mother, but I adored Lou Ann. I would do anything for that little girl – anything – and I did.

We walked back home. It was probably four miles or more. It was cold like only coastal rainy weather can be, scouring right into your bones. We had on rubber boots and rain jackets, but we were wet through and through. We held hands some of the time and we smoked cigarettes. Lou Ann could light a cigarette in a hurricane, so she lit them and handed them over to me. We didn't talk much. We saw one car coming and we made it over the edge of the ditch bank and into the underbrush without them seeing us. We sat there for a moment. I distinctly remember what Lou Ann said to me. She said, "You and I are gonna be fucked up, Carl. That old man just fucked us over again." She took a long drag on her cigarette and then she said, "But I love you, and I am always gonna love you. Always, forever, no matter what."

When she said that I wanted to grab her, kiss her and take care of her forever. But you knew Lou Ann as well as I did, and that is not how things happened. That was a slight crack in her shell and as soon as it was said, she closed back over and never let me hear those words again. Just like she did with everyone, she left you wanting more of her, but you could not have it. Nobody could.

May met us, nervous and fussing over our wellbeing. She had hot coffee for us and insisted on warm showers immediately. We put our clothes in the wash and settled in for a quiet breakfast in our warm kitchen. May cleaned our boots while we showered and erased any trace of our late-night ride. We ate our pancakes and talked about the weather, the upcoming sporting season, our wood supply, the weather some more.

Looking back, I realize that Lou Ann and I never asked May how she would survive financially without Earl. But I realized as the years went by that they had not spent any money, except on tobacco and booze and some food. There must have been savings. May also got his Social Security checks. May never talked about money, so I guess, we didn't think to ask her. I always worked from them on and I bought groceries, fixed her car, repaired the shed on the roof, that sort of thing. She never asked for money or offered to pay for anything, so I guess that all worked out.

Well, my dear girl, I don't know if you can make heads or tails of this part of my life, but I have told it the best I can. It is a human story, a tale that has played out before in other places with other families and other cultures. It is harsh and raw and now you know it. Now, let me tell you about Lou Ann's mother, as I heard it from Granny Parsons and May over the years.

Spring – Lou Ann's Mother

Lou Ann came from a little hippie gal named Spring. Spring was born Louisa Ann, but May never knew her by anything but Spring. She came from Santa Cruz to work and to roam. She hitchhiked from place to place, stayed wherever she could and did whatever she could get paid for. She had been a waitress, a housekeeper, a marijuana harvester in Humboldt County; she picked berries and swept floors. She liked to wear long dresses and boots and braided her red hair to keep it out of her way when she worked.

No one she met on the road knew she had a daughter. Spring would travel back to Santa Cruz to visit her sometimes. Her daughter lived with Spring's aunt, but no one knew that until later.

When Spring met May she was completely taken in by May's Native American mannerisms. She had never been around this kind of woman. May at that time lived with just me. Earl had left her, and she told Spring he would not be returning.

At first May was taken back by Spring's enthusiasm. Spring was a sparkling person. She had a lightness in her step, and she seemed to be able to experience pure joy without conditions attached. She wanted to learn some medicinal practices from May, but that took a great deal of time as May wrote nothing down and did not freely share. Sometimes when May saw Spring coming up the drive, she shut the door, threw the bolt and sat very still in her room. I sat beside her and was very still as well, just as May had taught me. Completely silent. But as time went on, May began to open the door when she saw Spring sauntering up the driveway.

Spring worked at the small grocery store and lived in various campers, backrooms, and tents around the area. She was crazy for embroidering flowers on anything she could—her skirts, her blouses, around any button hole, on her jeans, on her underwear, on anything. She loved to eat magic mushrooms once a month to "clear the cobwebs." She would build a shelter on the beach, as isolated as she could get, and she would spend her "trip" in the shelter, experiencing the pure joy of a psychedelic.

She smoked pot in a small clay pipe and rolled her own cigarettes. She traded shell necklaces and embroidered shirts for anything you would give her.

She stayed near May for about one year. It was a time of discovery and happiness for both of them. May did not have a daughter. Most women naturally have a need for a daughter, someone to share their female perspective, to see the world through their eyes. When she met Spring and finally let her in, that rush of sharing filled May with a new peace, one she didn't know was missing.

Spring had never had a real mother. Her mother was unavailable and prided herself on her inability to be burdened by the needs of an offspring. Spring had been born with a need for love and connection that was deep and powerful, like her need to be part of the earth. She searched for that connection and she found it in May.

They were a good match. Spring was curious to the point of aggressiveness. May was quiet to the point of isolation. It took time for them to reach each other. It was a precious and worthy time. Many days sitting at the cedar plank table with Spring embroidering and asking May countless questions. May prepared the fish for drying, assembled her dried herbs, cooked stews and answered with nods and sighs.

The kitchen filled with their energy. It smelled of their hair and their skin and their total connection. May fell in love with the gregarious girl, and Spring with the wise and smoky woman of the earth. They looked at each other and saw the best of themselves. Isn't that what true love is, without the sexual desire, just the desire to be connected?

Spring shared the grief of her childhood. She talked about the cold rooms, the emptiness of wealth, the shadow of her inconvenient existence. She talked about her feelings of abandonment and isolation. She never talked about the big house, the servants, the things that filled the house. She only told May that she grew up in Connecticut and that she was an only child and she would never return. Spring was like so many of the wandering youth of her time. She rejected the money, the status, the restrictions of wealth and "good breeding." She wanted connections to people, to the earth, to the wind and the sky. She was a blessed and lost little hippie chick.

May did not find that she needed to share her past. May was a woman of the moment, made of the earth, sky and sea: daughter of her ancestors, Running Bird. She was a listener, a healer and an unsophisticated resident of the earth. She did not have the need or desire to dissect or probe her past.

The past expressed itself in her present. She knew what she knew through a long and winding trail of knowledge, and it served her best as she expressed it in her daily rituals and practices. That is why May had such a hard time with her addictions. They were not an expression of her inner self but an escape from her earthly monsters, namely Earl.

Spring had been a constant for some time when May began to notice a change in Spring's health. She was paler and less talkative. May, in her way, waited to see what Spring would ask of her. One day she came to May's house and sat at the kitchen table. Her hands were shaking. She told May that she had been feeling very weak and tired and she could not eat without throwing up. She said she needed a doctor.

May sent her to Doc Jensen with a note. Doc Jensen and May had been close for years. He delivered me. She did things for him when she needed money, and he accepted smoked fish, fresh clams, homegrown vegetables and cannabis for payment when she sent me for shots.

Doc Jensen did some testing and sent Spring back to May. Spring had a fast-growing stomach cancer. It had gone too far for any treatment to stop it. She had only months to live. Spring and May sat in silence and held hands. Spring cried softly, and May looked at her beautiful face and saw the disease.

Spring talked about the early years, when she left her home at seventeen. She said she had not seen her parents since she left. As far as she knew, they had never tried to find her. She said returning to them now would be too painful. She could not take the disappointment, the rejection, the judgment.

She then told May that the free-love lifestyle she lived those first years had gifted her with a baby girl. She started to cry and shook her head back and forth. She said, "I tried so hard, May. I wanted her to have a good life. I thought I would be able to do that for her, but I just didn't know how to do it. I just wasn't ready and so I took her to my aunt in Santa Cruz." She went on to share that her aunt was a black sheep in her mother's family and had not been around any of the East Coast people for years. She lived in a big house in Santa Cruz with four sons and various lovers, mostly much younger than herself. She took in Spring and the baby, but she did not encourage them to make it their home.

Spring said one day she just took off without the baby, her daughter Lou Ann. She said she left a note that said, *I am on the move. I will return.* She said she tried to see Lou Ann every few months.

She thought she was safe with her aunt, but she knew the situation was not ideal. She had planned to try and bring her up to the Oregon Coast and make a life for them, but she hadn't done it yet.

She begged May to take the little girl. It was not an easy sell. May had many qualities and the many mysteries of earth and life hovered around her, but her mothering was buried under a heavy load. Childhood for May had been hard. You could see that in her movements and her face, though she never discussed it. Taking on a young girl was so much to ask.

May opened to people slowly and could close back into her shell, like a little snail, if she thought things were getting too close to her soul. Her intimacy was with her natural surroundings, not with the chatter of the human voice. May felt calm in a wild windstorm, lashing at the hillsides that rolled down to the turbulent ocean. She understood the groan of a tree or the roar of the surf better than she understood idle chatter and small talk. People were distracting, and the clamor of their voices made her shrink away.

The thought of another child was daunting. I had been delivered to her in a dream. She told me this. She saw me standing on a cliff with my head held high, sniffing the air as a bear cub will do. I rolled toward the ocean in the wet grass and swatted at the flies. I walked into the surf and I passed my paw through the incoming waves playfully. She felt herself hovering above me and heard my heart beating inside of her. When she woke up she knew I was coming. She understood this. This she could do. It did not take all of her strength, it just took her body and mind to carry the Boy Bear into this world. And so, she did.

But Spring wanted to bring a child, unknown to May. A child who was not anchored to her mother. A child without a face for May to study. She resisted mightily and spoke of the bonds that the child had already made with the redheads. But Spring was persuasive.

She described Lou Ann to May. She said her hair was yellow and gold with glinting red highlights. She said her eyes were as blue as the ocean when it is high summer and the waves are turquoise, just before they crest. She told her that Lou Ann was clever and could read everything. She was able to entertain herself for hours. She said she was a gift, a beautiful and intelligent little being that deserved more than the distracted great aunt and her numerous lovers. May gave in, and plans were made. This is how Lou Ann came to live in the House of Moses.

So, they plotted, and Spring returned to her aunt's home and told her a lie that she had a home for her and Lou Ann in Seattle. She still was not willing for anyone in her family to have access to little Lou Ann on a long-term basis. Her aunt looked her over suspiciously and said you had better get some rest and something to eat or you won't be taking care of anyone. Spring held it all together for a day and then she got on the bus with Lou Ann and headed back to May.

When May met Lou Ann, she was unsettled by her beauty. She was used to Spring's lightness of being, but the strawberry blonde child with the pale blue eyes was like a little angel. May brought me into the room to meet Lou Ann, and we fell in love with each other at first sight. I stared, and Lou Ann grabbed my hand and said, "Can we go out to play?"

As May and Spring looked out the window at the little ones – she told me later – Spring was certain that this was the way things needed to happen. Spring could not see into the future, but I always knew my mother withheld something from Lou Ann. She once told me that she dreamed of Lou Ann and she was broken like a little crab on the rocks. May said she knew then that Lou Ann should not have come, but it was too late. She had made her promise to Spring, and she could not break it.

While Spring was in Santa Cruz at her aunt's, May had made a powerful medicine for Spring. They sat for one last time at the cedar plank table and held hands. Then Spring kissed May's cheek and took one last look out the window at Lou Ann. She slipped out the back door and headed down the back path to the creek. She followed the creek to the ocean. She found the secluded little cove and the shelter that May had made for her. She sat and looked at the sunset over the water and listened to the waves and the shorebirds. She laid down on the cedar bows and took the medicine and was dead within twenty-four hours.

When they found her, she didn't have any identification on her. Some people recognized her from the store, but no one knew her real name or where her family was. She was buried by the County as an unknown. Her grave was marked by an etched rock that read, "Spring Lies Here." It was one of May's creations.

This was never shared with Lou Ann. None of it. She believed her mother was a junkie. That is how Spring wanted it. She did not want Lou Ann to search and find her family. She did not want her to feel the deep rejection she had felt from her parents and the conditional love she had felt from her aunt. She wanted her to become May's daughter.

I think I should have told Lou Ann that her mother was a different person than May led her to believe. Maybe knowing something like that would have help ground her. She really was loved by Spring. Even though Spring made a bad choice, she did it for love, to protect her little girl. But I did not tell her, and that is not something I feel good about. I should have told her.

Spring had an idea of Lou Ann growing up in the rolling hills beside the beautiful Pacific Ocean. She romanticized the life of a little girl, running free with her Native stepmother and her stepbrother. She saw her growing up like a little wildflower. She never saw what would happen. How could she?

As far as May knew, no one from Spring's family inquired after her. May would have remained silent and done her best to keep Lou Ann. She had promised. She would watch over Little Wave. But no one ever came and looked for Spring.

Lou Ann and I lived the life Spring wanted for her daughter for a few blissful years. They ran and played in the outdoors. We were best friends, and May kept us safe. May had her weakness for alcohol, but when we were small, and Earl was gone, we were her center. She even moved us all up to Astoria for a year when she got word that she could get free room and board and take care of a wealthy woman, Mrs. Bonham. The three of us moved there for a year and used the money Earl sent to keep the coast house. We stayed until it was time for us kids to go to school, and then we returned to the old place.

Chapter 39

Leah

They did not see my future the way I did. College, universities, careers...none of those things were part of me yet. Sometimes a kid is born and says from age two, "I want to be an engineer," and at twenty-five, he is one. Everybody wants that kid, but there aren't many, and I wasn't one of them.

My inner voice said go out and live your life and embrace it. I wanted to work at a job, pay bills, sit by the ocean when I could, find the pieces of myself that were strung up and down the coastline.

There was no danger that I would turn to prostitution or abusive men. I had already seen those, and I was not made of that stuff.

My fear was of addiction because the only person I'd knew anything about who was family had abandoned me for drugs. It could have been my father and/or my mother, but whoever left me was either an addict or insane. Strange how much that can haunt you, the not knowing.

Insanity was a lesser fear because I just felt centered. Sharon said it was my natural way of being. Somehow, in the midst of my unconventional and dangerous and chaotic life, I had found my center of gravity. Uncle Carl said it was a gift from a higher power. I don't know if I believe that, but when I left "home," I was in pretty good mental health.

That first year with Uncle Carl and Aunt Sharon was bittersweet. Lou Ann had been a complex mother and as much as I loved her, some of the things she put me through began to surface. One thing that started happening was stealing. There was a certain satisfaction I felt in it. I was very good at it.

At first, I picked up small things when Sharon and I went out. I took things I thought Lou Ann might need: shampoo, lacey undies, a glittery hair clip, red lipstick. My awareness that this was unacceptable was clear, so I stored them in a box I had in my closet that contained a few of Lou Ann's things.

Sometimes I forgot and stole two beers. I didn't like it, so I poured it down the toilet and snuck the cans out to the garbage. Aunt Sharon let me have Pepsi, which I still preferred warm, but sometimes I stole some of that too.

Aunt Sharon did not say anything at first. One day we had an afternoon together and we were just sitting. Sharon did not sit. She was busy all the time. We were sitting because she had a bad cold. She was lying on the couch with a blanket, and I was reading to her. We were reading *The Lord of the Rings* Trilogy. We were taking a break and she said, "You are like a Hobbit, Leah."

"I am not so short!"

"I mean your ability to slip past clerks in the store. You are a good thief, like a Hobbit."

I was quiet, and she continued. "You will get caught some time. The penalty isn't too bad, but it will be embarrassing. Did you ever get caught before?"

"No. I have been doing it since I can remember."

"Well, you had to then, right? Why do you do it now?"

"It makes me feel like some things are still the same."

"Like Lou Ann is still here?" I was silent. How could I hurt Sharon by saying I missed Lou Ann, the fuckup who brought me here? Sharon went on. "It makes sense to me, Leah. You were taught and have a knack for it, like if you had been taught a second language or something. Yeah, like it is your second language. But you know, you gotta ask yourself, is this a talent, a habit, or an attempt to keep Lou Ann's memory? When you figure that out maybe you can replace it with something else."

I said, "Okay."

And then she said, "I need to sleep now, honey."

As I went upstairs, I tried to sort out what she just gave me. I started to think that Aunt Sharon was my Gandalf, my wizard. This was how she dispensed words of wisdom. There was no lecture or judgment. She just shined a light, put a mirror in front of you and let you do your own thing. It was a good technique with me; I had control of my own life for the first time.

The stealing slowed down, but I still do it now as an adult. Not like I did before, but I help myself to small things. I just like to see if I still have it. My second language.

Another consequence of my upbringing was the constant change I was accustomed to. In a home you stay in there are repeated sounds that people just become used to. Like the sound of a door closing, how the back-gate latch sounds, how your neighbor's garage door sounds, your coffee pot, the mailbox opening. I was not used to that sameness. It got under my skin some days and I found myself irritated and feeling trapped. Eventually, the sameness brought comfort, but in retrospect, I had a lot of anxiety about it. I never wanted to appear ungrateful. I was always afraid just a little that I could be plucked out of this safe world I had landed in. Just an old habit from years of uncertainty.

None of us were used to the idea of our family. We were teaching ourselves as we went along. Sometimes we just fell flat. Carl had an idea that we should "build new memories" through sports, and he came on pretty strong. We tried shooting hoops in the driveway, bowling, golfing, swimming, game night, and movie night with sports-themed movies. Aunt Sharon saw that I was stressed by his need to clean my slate, so to speak, so she intervened. She stated we were just going to let our memories happen. Uncle Carl and I both felt relief.

We did enjoy the ocean, all of us. We found we liked it rain or shine and in any season. We lived close enough to go often. We collected driftwood, stones, and occasional shells. We started a little back porch display, which we incorporated with the old furniture that was out there. We added little twinkle lights, a lantern, a soft homemade braided rug, pillows, colored glass bottles with sand and tiny shells. We had a little bookshelf full of paperbacks. We built that memory, and it came easy. It created its own space in each of us, quiet but cheerful. We all spent time together there and time alone too.

I made a little traveling replica of that memory and each apartment or old house I lived in I had it on display. I made a shadow box out of two old wooden boxes and they were filled with assorted sea treasures. I always put a red lipstick tube of Lou Ann's on one of the shelves.

At eighteen, I thought I should leave and make my own way. I had finished my home-school program and even taken a year of classes at the local community college, but I hadn't found what I was looking for, like how I wanted to make money. I moved to a studio apartment in Newport and started work as a waitress at an oceanside diner. The pay was minimum wage, plus tips. At least once a week, Carl and Sharon ventured in to eat on one of my dinner shifts. Still hovering, but no interference. Once I told them what I was doing, they helped out by getting me some housewares and moved my stuff in Carl's truck. I didn't drive at the time, so I just took a bicycle. I didn't plan to go far.

My boss, Nelda, had owned the place for twenty-five years. She was a working drunk, always sipping whiskey in a coffee cup, but never any signs she was too drunk to function. The place was clean, lots of regulars and an occasional tourist. It was a good place to learn.

My apartment was across the street in an old three-story wooden building. At one time it was a tavern below, with rooms to rent above. Its name then was "Betty's Burgers and Beds." Big Betty, all 350 pounds of her, rented the rooms mostly to prostitutes and fisherman. I had lived there once with Lou Ann and returning was just part of my journey. Now it was just Ocean View Apartments.

We lived there when I was about eight or nine years old. Betty would let girls rent a room on a weekly basis. No questions, never be late with rent and above all no kids. Lou Ann was cagey; she found a way to hide me and still turn tricks.

We rented a back room on the third floor. The room came with a small bathroom, a double bed, a closet, a dresser, and a braided rug. We had a window that looked out on an empty lot, choked with weeds.

If the other women found out I was there they would have got Lou Ann's ass kicked out. That is what Lou Ann told me. Competition could be wicked, and red-blonde hair was one of her moneymakers. I figured this all out over time, but when we were there I knew what to do to avoid detection.

Lou Ann slept in the daytime. Blanket over the window, snuggled up until sunset. I snuck around the building, visited neighboring stores to steal lunch, went to the beach and dodged adults. Sometimes I stayed in the room and read a magazine I found in the trash or a newspaper or drew pictures. Lou Ann got up and around at 5:00. She drank a couple beers with her first cigarettes. Then she would go down to Betty's and get milk and something for us to split. We loved the fried clams the most.

Lou Ann would dress for her job. Everything was skin tight and low-cut. Her makeup was heavy, and her blue eyes sparkled.

She always said, "You've got about thirty minutes, kid." As soon as the door shut I arranged my bed in the closet. I had a cozy little setup with a pillow, blankets and a padded mattress Lou Ann had snuck up to our room. I got in my bed, slid the doors shut and put in ear plugs and some ear muffs we had picked up at the Value Village. I drank the Nyquil she gave me out of a little bottle, curled up and slept. I was like a little trained monkey.

No sounds could come out of the closet. "Do not come out of the closet no matter what you hear. When the doors slide open, you can climb in bed with me. Not a sound, you hear me? They will take you away, kid, and I don't know where you will end up." I heard that every day of my life until I got to Uncle Carl's.

We lasted there for a while, maybe it was a couple of months. It all ended when something hit the closet doors hard enough to wake me. I pulled off my ear muffs and pulled out my ear plugs. I could hear Lou Ann saying, "Please, no, please, that's too much, please no."

I tried to stay put, but I heard the crunch of what I knew was a fist on a face. (Another thing I learned in childhood.) I slid the closet door open a crack and saw a big hairy back looming over Lou Ann, who was trying to get off the bed. I was quick, and I was stealthy. I aimed for his head and hit it full force with a can of warm Pepsi. Then, as he turned, Lou Ann hit him with the lamp. We were both on top of him, biting, kicking and basically riding him like a bull. Lou Ann had always told me that if someone attacked me, I was to poke their eyes out and scream bloody murder. In the mayhem, I managed to jab one finger in his eye, bit his ear and scratch his face. Lou Ann knocked him out with her second swing of the bedside lamp. It was high drama.

Big Betty was at the door in her robe, panting, in a few minutes. She said, "We'll drag him out back, then you and the kid get out." Then she grabbed the $50 on the dresser and turned to me and said, "You grab his feet, kid." She yelled down the hallway, "Leo, get your ass up here and help me!" Her little bald-headed husband appeared instantly. Lou Ann, Leo, and Leah, we were the assigned crew. We dragged him to the back lot and rolled him into the tangled weeds among various abandoned pieces of cars, wood, and garbage.

Lou Ann and I did one of our quick packing jobs and were out the door and headed north via Lou Ann's thumb within fifteen minutes of the body dump. Lou Ann had a black eye and a loose tooth. In the street light with blinking neon, she was a frightening vision. She had a wild look in her eyes; she could not stop grinning and then sneering. I didn't even know if she knew I was beside her until she opened a can of beer, chugged it, and grabbed my hand. We left Newport again, for the umpteenth time. And now I was back, but for what, I didn't know.

My new room in Newport was small and it faced the ocean. The diner was a one-story building, so my third-floor room was flooded with the changing light of the coastline. The windows were not clear. The sea salt had pitted them, and the moisture leaked in, but the ocean was there. It still gave off its own light: gray, then white, darker, then turquoise blue. It was good. The new owner who bought Betty's had done some renovations and the whole building was apartments now. My room had a new carpet and new shower. Otherwise it was mostly the same.

My new boss told me Betty had finally died at sixty-one years old, completely bedridden because of her weight. Leo had to arrange for an ambulance to move them to a small house out of town. Rumor was it took five men with straps to get her on a gurney. She died shortly after that. She said Leo is still alive, and I actually saw him at the diner.

He looked the same. He weighed maybe 125 pounds, about 5'3". He looked in good health, and he ordered the special, clam chowder in a bread bowl. I asked to take a break and then asked him if I could sit down. He said, "Sure," and I slipped into his booth. I wasn't sure what I wanted to say to Leo. How do you start the kind of conversation that was an attempt to gain information and be anonymous? How do you say you are chasing memories, looking for clues and not sound like a weirdo? So I just said, "I was sorry to hear Betty passed away. My mother and I rented from her about ten years ago."

He looked at me closely and said, "Big Betty didn't let children stay in the rooms." Then he winked and chuckled. I ventured on. "Do you remember the guy we dragged out to the weed patch?"

He put his spoon down, looked closer and said, "You and your mama banged up old Joe Hawkins pretty bad. He went blind in one eye over that. Good thing he's dead now, honey, or you could be in danger." Then he chuckled again. "Where's your mama now?"

"Dead five years now."

"Oh, I am so sorry to hear that. She was a beauty, but kind of crazy, right?"

"If prostitutes are crazy, in general, I guess, but she also was smarter than most people I have known."

"Oh honey, I'm sorry. I shouldn't have said that. She was doing her best, I am sure."

I smiled at Leo and said, "My break is over. I'll see you next time, I hope."

He looked at me with a puzzled expression, then he grinned and chuckled, "Why sure you will, honey."

That night I could not stop pondering Leo's words. I had never realized that Betty knew kids were staying there, but really how could she miss it? And she never turned Lou Ann into authorities, and no one came for me, ever. Maybe Lou Ann was crazy; well, she was crazy. She let men beat her;

she hid a child and never let me go to school or see my only relatives. What was Lou Ann thinking? Was it complex or simple? Was I her little girl in her heart or her little sister?

Was I the excuse she needed to keep up the wandering? Was I precious to her or convenient? Why did she take me? She could have taken me to a hospital or a shelter and left me. What was my place in her life? The reality of having no identity had always been an issue, especially difficult as I matured. But hearing someone other than Carl or Sharon talk about Lou Ann was unnerving. It made me feel like I had a big hole in my body I could not fill. *Just who in the hell was I?* I started to panic, and I didn't know how to calm down. I called Aunt Sharon.

Chapter 40

Sharon

Our own Little Wave was on a journey. She needed to find some answers. Her first years at our house were a rest period for her tender little heart. She was overexposed to the worst of life and hungry for peace. She didn't ask as many questions as we thought she would, and neither did we. We all just existed in our little world of family, and we didn't break the spell. We stayed in an unnamed circle, and it helped us heal, or so we believed. When Carl shared some of the family history (murder and mystery), Leah took it in, but still seemed at peace. It was where she was at the time – safe – and no amount of information was going to interfere with that safety.

We were all healing from all kinds of pain. We were all vulnerable but unwilling to show it. We understood where we were, and we stayed there. It was safe. But it had to change. Leah changed it for all of us, and it was good. She jarred us back to reality when she wanted to go back to her past to find her way forward.

We worried at first. Here was a bright kid with all the brains to pull out of this coastal life. She was very intelligent and enjoyed learning. I saw her in an office, her secretary arranging her schedule, her hair in a bun with important meetings and reports all around her.

But Leah was still rolling in and out to sea with nothing to hold onto but the rhythm of her unresolved past. She chose to understand. How could we try to stop her from doing that?

The job in Newport felt like a good start. She wasn't too far away, and we knew Nelda. She would teach her the trade. She was no-nonsense and hardworking. Leah would start out with a solid step.

The call that night of her first crisis was a surprise, but not bad news to me. She had to begin somewhere, and Carl and I didn't have the road map.

She was gasping for air and when she spoke it was hard to understand her. Then I heard, "Why did she keep me? Why did she take me with her? Why would she let a child live that life?" More choked sobs…

"Breathe deep and slow and breathe into a paper bag, Leah. Just concentrate on breathing and slow it down. Yes, that's it, just slow your breathing down. It is okay, it is time for you to ask these questions. It is okay. You aren't alone, honey. We are right with you."

When she could speak she sounded so small. "Thank you. I'm just exhausted with all these feelings. I don't know what to do, but I'm so glad I can call you."

When we hung up, I saw her in my mind. Her long dark hair, those beautiful eyes, her slender build. I saw the future too. Long periods of suffering, discovering, maybe running. I wanted to give her answers, but I didn't have them. I didn't understand why Lou Ann took a child on a prostitute's journey.

Lou Ann could have had other jobs, but she couldn't stay still, and she wanted the pain of physical abuse. She was a victim when she was a young girl, but in adulthood, she faced her abusers with the courage she couldn't have had at twelve or thirteen. She kept control to some degree, but why the child? Why?

When I told Carl, he just went to the guilt place. It pissed me off. Why let the guilt lock him into that place of self-pity? Fuck Earl and May! They were the guilty ones. And the strung-out mother and God knows who else that influenced and fucked up Lou Ann and in turn Leah.

Leah called the next morning to let me know she was doing better. But we both knew there would be more.

Chapter 41

Leah

When Lou Ann died, I had felt very sad, but I also had felt relief. Now I could finally say it, after five years; Lou Ann was a burden. She held me down, and I stayed chained to her like the stray that I was. The farther I moved away from my childhood, the harder it was to bear.

Let's start with hunger. Why wasn't there food all the time? She always made money, cash. Lou Ann thought food was dangerous, dulled the senses. That's what she said. "Lean and mean, Leah. Fat and lazy. No way. Stay a little hungry."

The food I did steal was junk, but I didn't know any better. I was really hungry all the time, and I didn't like how it made me feel. I felt empty and scared. But Lou Ann was usually sleeping or working when

I ate that junk. What did she think I was doing? She must have trusted me. But I was so little.

I remembered things about our life together. When the memories chose to come wasn't always a good time, but I had no control over it. It was like grief. It lived inside me always, and if it wanted to come out, it just did. It was not my call.

I was doing my laundry in the laundromat. I had the place to myself on a Saturday night. I was reading a book when the door swung open and a young woman stumbled in with her clothes and a little boy about three. She looked rough: stringy hair, bad teeth, nicotine fingers. She was skinny and had on a pair of denim short shorts and a ripped t-shirt. The little boy had matted hair and a crusty nose. He climbed under one of the tables and lay down. He had big empty eyes. He stuck his thumb in his mouth and was quiet. I couldn't take my eyes off of him. I knew a trained monkey when I saw one. She didn't look at him and filled her machine and went outside for a smoke. He fell asleep.

When she came back in, she looked at me and squinted and said, "What's up?"

I had not planned on talking to her, but suddenly I was, and it was like I could not stop myself.

"How old is your boy?"

"Three."

"He's a quiet little man."

"Damn right."

"Got any more?"

"Nope, just him. He wasn't even supposed to happen, but what the fuck. Sometimes you get caught, right? You ever been caught?"

"No."

"Lucky. Kids are expensive."

"Where do you work?"

"What? I don't have a day job. I'm on welfare mostly. Pick up a buck or two sometimes. Not steady…"

"Who watches him when you work?"

"Nobody. He stays with me."

"Do you clean houses?"

"Ha! Good one… No, I don't clean houses. (Pause) I suck dicks, okay?"

"My mother did that job too. Hard way to make a buck. But somebody is always willing to pay."

"Yeah, most the time. Hey, you ever take it up?"

"No. I saw enough. It's too risky."

"Yeah. It's not what you'd call a safe way to work. But I didn't need trainin' to do it."

"Aren't you worried about the boy?"

"Look, either I do it or we lose our place. Anyway, kids forget. He's a tough little guy."

I stopped myself right then. Had I forgotten all I had seen or was it still there? Did I have a dark box of awful memories buried deep inside? I left the laundromat abruptly with my clothes still damp.

At the apartment I laid my clothes over chairs and hung them everywhere to dry. Then I sat down and stared right into my past.

When did I realize what Lou Ann was doing? Was I scared? Did she keep it away from me most of the time? My first memories are of being alone in the dark. I had something that smelled like Lou Ann in my arms. A sweater, I think. I slept in the dark.

Then she would come in, and I would lie next to her. If men were there early on, I cannot remember.

Of course, there is the memory of staying in the closet at Betty's Burgers and Beds. But my memory of throwing open the closet door didn't include shock at Lou Ann's nudity or the man's nudity either.

So, somehow, I knew. It was normal to me. The swollen jaws, black eyes, bruised arms and split lips, I am not so sure about. Were they just like the sex? Just part of Lou Ann's work?

All I really knew of anything outside our world I read in magazines and newspapers or paperbacks I found in laundromats. I don't think I related to the news or stories. They were more like a dream world, fiction, and my reality was my life with Lou Ann.

Something wouldn't let me remember or else it was a non-event. I just couldn't get a feeling for it. I just felt numb. There was nothing to grab onto. I tried to be still and listen to my inner voice. It was like white noise roaring in my ears and I could not hear what might be in my head. Crying was not helpful, and I couldn't make myself do it. There was no relief, no release of the pain.

Part of me wanted to run home to Carl and Sharon. But more of me still needed answers. I wanted to know who I was, how I became this person and what could I do with all that information. It was like when I finally went to college in my early thirties. It was all-consuming study. Research, remembering, problem-solving, immersion in subjects. Just like college, I wanted good grades and good grades meant good information. Solid learning that would put me in a position to be successful. I guess you could say it was like going to twelve years of school, but the experiences were not spread out. They were concentrated and intense. It was a rocky time in my life.

Nelda was good to me. She let me work as much as I wanted, and she didn't ask me questions, past or present. Her only concern seemed to be my lack of friends, especially males.

I overheard her talking to her sister Dora in the kitchen one morning. Dora baked all of Nelda's pies and desserts. They were loading pies in the walk-in cooler and didn't see me in the back room.

Nelda was in mid-sentence. "Look at her, she is a beauty. She such a nice kid, but you know Lou Ann must have really messed with her head."

Dora said, "No boyfriend, no flirting? I mean come on. There aren't too many cute girls around here."

Nelda chuckled in her smoke-hardened way and said, "Dora, she doesn't even notice them. Barry just about drools when Leah waits on him, but she doesn't pay him any mind."

"Well, it won't last forever. She's gonna wake up and look in the mirror one day, and she'll be ready."

I didn't hear Nelda for a moment and then she said, "Maybe she's scared. I hear Lou Ann liked to be knocked around. Maybe Leah just thinks men come at you swingin'. I don't know."

I heard the cooler close. They went back into the kitchen. I stepped out of the building and breathed in the sea air. Fuck it.

That night I took inventory of myself. Hair, long and wavy, kind of a chestnut brown. Skin, clear, light in color. Teeth straight and white. Eyes, unusual blue, fairly large. Nose, small and rounded on the end. Body, slim, but curvy hips and breasts, tummy flat, legs not too long. Height, 5'5". Weight 126 pounds. All in order.

Had I noticed men and boys looking at me? Yes, but I wasn't looking back. Why? Didn't I like it? Did I want something from them? No. It meant nothing to me. Did I have to feel something? Or had "Lou Ann really messed up my head," like Nelda said?

The only thing I knew right then was that I could not deal with anyone but myself. I was aware I looked good, that I fit the American ideal of beauty. It felt like a curse. I wanted to blend in and go about my business, but this "beauty" was a burden. So, I just shut off the attention.

I wore simple and plain clothes; jeans, t-shirts (four for $20 at Fred Meyer), hair in a pony, running shoes, hoodies, occasionally a raincoat. No makeup, no jewelry. No red lipstick and glitter. No red bras and lacey panties. Nothing that a prostitute would need. Nearly invisible, which I knew how to do.

And then there was the fact that Nelda knew Lou Ann and she knew who I was…what? Did she know me when I was little? How does she know me now? It was getting harder to be Leah. Lou Ann was all around me.

Chapter 42

Leah – On the Move

I worked for Nelda for a couple of years. She was good to me and helped me get a job at another place up the coast at Seaside. She didn't ask why I was leaving, but she said I could always come back.

The new place was so busy in the summer that I had to get used to lots of co-workers and lots of families. The owners were a couple, Nancy and Ben, and they were always right there working beside us. The place had a bar, and Nancy was the main bartender. Ben ran the till out front and made the schedules.

I found a small trailer to live in with a little attached porch. It was in a small trailer court that Ben's brother owned. Rent was low, and once I got the mice under control, I felt at ease there.

Seaside brought back lots of memories. I found the little trailer we lived in, but it was just a shell now, windows busted out. The diner Lou Ann worked at was still open. It had new owners and a new front façade and flowers in planter boxes.

Carl and Sharon were farther away, but the ties were still strong. Uncle Carl brought me a scooter to ride around town. He insisted I get bright yellow and a yellow helmet. I loved that scooter.

It was during my time in Seaside that I met Bernie. He was really handsome: curly black hair, big brown eyes and a mouth full of white teeth. It didn't hurt that he smiled all of the time. He that cheerful self-assured way about him that comes from good looks and a nice body.

We met in the restaurant. He was in Seaside for the summer, staying at his grandparents' summer home. He was a student at the University of Washington, wealthy family, silver spoon type. He was an experiment for me. What would it be like to flirt and banter with a male?

My whole experience that two years away was like that. I felt like a voyeur, disconnected emotionally, but interested in other people's motives and emotions.

Bernie (Bernard Alexander Brighton) liked to play at being a vegetarian, a minimalist, a nature boy. He didn't let me know he was from a wealthy family at first, trying to avoid being stereotyped. But unfortunately, no matter how hard we try, humans tend to fit each other in boxes.

He had lots of questions for me. It seemed to all be part of his little act, being interested in someone other than himself. I kept up without revealing any of my past. I grew up inland, Portland to be exact. I was taking a year off just to work before I returned to Portland State. That was all easy. I had a good idea what that life would look like.

The first time we went somewhere we walked the beach. Bernie was fun to look at and he was funny. I held his hand and I let him kiss me. It went like this, "Leah, you are gorgeous, do you know that?

I said, "Sure. You just told me."

He said, "And you are funny too. Come here."

The kiss was nice. It was my first real kiss, but I seemed to know exactly how to do it. It felt natural. Bernie tasted delicious and his cheeks were smooth above his rough jaw line. I looked in his eyes and saw that "man need," and I felt nauseous. I pulled back and he said, "What's up, pretty Leah?"

I lied and said, "I liked that. Thanks."

He gasped, "Thanks? Okay so let me try it again and see what you say."

I laughed and started running. We chased each other around the beach for a while and then walked back with our arms around each other.

That night I lay in bed and tried to imagine what it would be like to have Bernie next to me. I explored my body and gave myself an orgasm. I had learned to do that by reading magazines. It was relaxing, but I never thought about a man or a woman when I did it. I just chased the climax. It was enough.

The next date was a drive to Astoria and dinner. We took his car. It was a sports car and it prompted me to ask more about him. On that date, we talked about his family. They were wealthy, living on Mercer Island on Lake Washington. His mother was Jewish, an East Coast transplant. His father had moved to Washington from Britain. He was the only child and had lived a very privileged life. He could not walk away from the money, but he was trying to find himself, just like I was. It made me realize that having all the puzzle pieces in place still doesn't eliminate the need to make your own story. It was just different.

That night he came to my little trailer, and we tried out sex. I had watched enough television and movies by then and I knew how to respond but it was pretty much just an act. Lou Ann kept appearing in my head as we did the deed. I could not keep myself from thinking about how many times she had done it and with how many hundreds of men. It was all for the man in my mind. It sickened me, but I had this need to experience it.

When he rolled over all sweaty and satisfied, he kissed my cheek and fell sound asleep. I lay there feeling his semen drip down my leg and thought I would like to avoid this act as much as possible in my life. Maybe never again would be just fine.

The next time I saw Bernie he seemed shallow and even his smile didn't hold any charm. Again, I acted more interested than I was, but I avoided any more dates. He was just looking for fun and he had all the means to get it, so there was no drama. Bye, Bernie.

Life in Seaside was pretty good for a while. I met a girl.

When I had lived with Sharon, she introduced me to Carla. The only reason that didn't work was simply that we could not really relate to each other. Carla was kind of strange, but Carla's life was very "normal." Mom, Dad, cat, dog, little brother, house on a street in a small town where you had always lived. She was sweet and that was pleasant, because back then kindness felt so good. I was feeling safe and I wanted to give my love to people around me then. The doors in my heart were still open. I was still a little girl. I was still filled with awe at the new life I came into. Isolation was my past then. I was into connection.

But Carla was just a little experience, and when she left for college we hugged and waved good-bye. We promised to keep in touch, but again, we were marginally close, and I only heard about her through Sharon after that.

My new friend was a waitress whom I met at work. Her name was Amy. She grew up in Long Beach, Washington. She was a rough and rowdy girl, tattoos and black eyeliner. She smoked a lot. I spent a lot of time with her for a few months. I even found myself giving her some information about my upbringing, a watered-down version. We had some things in common. We both grew up with very little money in crappy places on the coast with mothers who were unreliable.

We laughed a lot. She was very promiscuous, and she loved to share stories about all of her experiences. I was living them through her, so I didn't have to do it myself. She had a great sense of freedom and she loved to be spontaneous. I had more fun with her than anyone before or since. She had the Lou Ann quality of living in the moment and I had missed that part of Lou Ann because frankly, I do not possess that quality.

Once Amy had "screwed" two boys at once. She described it to me and I excused myself to throw up in the bathroom. She was very cavalier about the whole thing. It seemed like sex was just like eating for her. You need to do it to stay alive. I could not relate, but the stories were still fascinating. She didn't do it for money like Lou Ann. She did it because she liked it and she thought men were stupid and funny when they did it. She would describe their bodies and make fun of them. She talked about how they thought she was so "hot", but she knew she was just easy. She was the coolest person I ever met.

Amy told me about the time her "bitch of a Mother" sent her to stay with the next-door neighbors while she ran off with one of her trucker boyfriends. Amy laughed when she told me about it, but it was awful. They were as poor as her and her Mom and they had three other children already living in their single wide trailer. She was asked to sleep on the floor, in the hallway by the bathroom on a little mat they made for her out of old clothes. Everything else in the house was covered with junk and garbage. She said the other kids slipped into their slots on mattresses on the floor, piled high with old clothes, shoes, blankets and everything smelling of mildew and dog shit, because of course there were 4 dogs in that house too. She told me that the smells were the worst and she felt like they got into her sinuses and everywhere she went and everything she ate smelled like that horrible trailer. When I asked her how old she was, it was amazing how she counted her childhood years, very similar to the way I do. She said, "I think I had lost my front teeth and I know we weren't in school because they sent us home with lice and the woman who was "taking care" of us just said, fuck it you are staying home." She lived there for what she thought was a couple of months. When her Mom came back they left. She had failed to pay rent on their trailer. Amy said she always moved in garbage bags too, but she had toys she took with her. I felt some envy, as weird as that may seem. I did not really recall any toys, just some tattered books.

We spent most of our time off together for those few months. We bought cigarettes and some kind of liquor and sat on the seawall and laughed and drank. Like me, Amy still loved the beach even though we had spent all of our lives on it. We built bonfires at night and drank until we were stumbling. Sometimes on our day off we would drive in her old car down to Lincoln City and watch people fly kites or sit in the car in the rain and eat greasy fries and clams. Whatever we were doing it felt great. I had never had anyone like Amy in my life. We never missed work and we never missed an opportunity to run free. When I think back on that time, I see her shiny black hair pulled up into a bun on her head and her black eyeliner expertly drawn above her big brown eyes. I think I looked at her constantly. She never said anything about it, but she never let me get too close physically. She had experience. She knew what could happen. I didn't until it was too late for me to try.

I let Amy in on some of my past in a different way than anyone else. I told her isolated stories and I didn't make them quite as dark as they were in real life. She loved the story of my stay at Mrs. Bonham's and her ghost husband. It was so nice to see it through her eyes. It changed the perspective.

My time at Mrs. Bonham's was a gift, a real adventure. It almost made me want to forgive Lou Ann.

I didn't tell her the worst, but I did describe some of the spots we lived in. Her spots were so similar, I didn't have to describe them in the detail that I would have to for someone who had always had a home, in the same place, with food in the cupboards and your own shower. She had seen the same used up trailers and apartments that I had seen. She had not experienced the abandoned shacks and the warehouses, but she knew people who had lived in them. Sometimes we marveled that we did not ever meet each other. She did not know that I was kept hidden and that I never went to school. I tried to tell her, but it stuck in my throat. I didn't want any pity from her. I just wanted someone to relate to.

I was really thinking I wanted to tell her more about myself and maybe even suggest we share an apartment. But she up and left. She met an older guy with some money and a nice car and he wanted to take her to California. I tried to tell her that he was just using her, but she said, "Oh duh, and I am using him back! I want to get off this coastline, baby. California is calling me!"

My heart broke. I thought she was going to be in my life. I thought I would be talking to her for the rest of my life. I thought I had connected with her and she felt the same. I had already seen us as old women, on a porch, laughing and smoking and talking about the good old days when we were waitresses. I didn't even realize I had done that until she said she was leaving. How did this happen? Why does she want to leave? I was thinking I could be enough for her. She was enough for me, more than I could ever hope for. How did this happen, I just kept repeating that in my head, over and over.

She dropped by to see me the day she left. She gave me a leather bracelet she had made me that said "Leah, Love, Life." She hugged me good-bye and said, "Wish me luck, Blue Eyes!" As she pulled away from me, I felt the floor swallow me whole. I sunk into deep sadness for days. I know now that I loved her. It was just too damn much for me. That kind of loss, again, it just wasn't going to work for me. It pulled the guts out of me.

I walked in a trance for weeks. I was going through the motions, work, home, work, but I felt wrecked in a new way. I didn't even want to tell anyone. First, she was supposed to just be a friend, but she was more. I wasn't even sure if I was a lesbian or just lonely. It all just felt horrible. I think it was the first time I had ever fully felt the impact of loss. Weird, as I had lost so much already in life, but most of that was just done to me. Amy was different. I had sought her out, and deep inside I think I thought that would make it easier. But, of course, it didn't.

If I wanted to live, I had to avoid those connections, those painful experiences. Otherwise, I knew I was too fragile. The uncharted waters of my soul, deep recesses of pain, were best to avoid at all costs. Protecting myself was my job now, and I was going to do it in a way no one else could. It was my brand, my shield, my power.

Then I met a woman named Janice who was connected to my past. Janice was a regular at the bar. Every day about 11:00 a.m. she came in, newspaper in hand, ordered clam chowder and coffee. After she read the paper she switched to whiskey shots, consuming three by 2:00 p.m. and off she went. Just part of her routine.

Janice knew lots of people. She worked at the grocery store from 6:00 to midnight, five days a week. She had the look of a woman who was probably always noticed for her figure when she was younger. Some women never give up; if their looks worked for them once, they still try to use them. She wore her pants skin-tight, dyed her hair jet black and painted her eyebrows black. She reminded me of what Lou Ann might have turned into if she had lived.

Janice had a husky smoker voice, long red nails and blue eyeshadow. She smoked out back with the cook, and she blew the smoke out of her nostrils after she inhaled it with that curling motion only long-time smokers can pull off.

All these observations were mine because I recognized her. She had been someone Lou Ann would step out with some evenings. She always called Janice her buddy, but as usual, she kept her away from me, and I would watch them through a crack in the curtains as they walked uptown to the bars.

At first, I just observed Janice without contact. Then I started going into the store she worked in several days a week. She recognized me from the restaurant, and we started a friendly banter.

I felt very calculating. I never made friends. I was not well versed in the art of casual acquaintances, but I wanted to get information, so I acted out the role, and I must say I thought I was very good at deception.

Janice and I had breakfast a couple of times for starters. They were my days off, and we went to Lou Ann's old diner. It was off season, so it was quieter, mostly locals. My inquiries were measured as I did not want to seem too obsessed with Janice's life. I found out she was born right there and had only lived near here, except for a short stint in Long Beach, Washington, up north. She had married a guy, but he was a bum who stole her car and left her penniless, so she came back home.

I made up my past for her. It was pretty mundane, my ploy to discourage questions. Apparently, I was raised in the Umpqua Valley by my parents, Fred and Diane. I was an only child, with a peaceful childhood on a small farm where Fred and Diane still live. I had horses and dogs, and after I graduated from high school, I went into waitressing. End of story.

Then I told another lie to move us to the topic of Lou Ann. I told Janice my mother had strawberry blonde hair and pale blue eyes. That broke the ice. Janice smiled. "I knew a gal who had that same coloring. She was wild and crazy, Lou Ann. She was a looker too. I heard she was killed a few years ago. Some asshole she took up with, I guess. Tragic, she was such a beauty."

"What did she do?"

Janice chuckled, "Well a little of this and a little of that. We worked right here together for a while."

"So, a waitress, huh?"

"Oh no, no, no. Lou Ann was a hooker. She was pretty well known along the coast. I guess she took straight jobs sometimes." She paused and looked into her coffee. "She was very strange, but I liked her. She didn't seem to be completely there, but she was a happy gal. She would do anything they asked her to do. I guess getting beat up was one of her trademark services. I just couldn't figure that one out."

I asked, "Was she always alone?"

"Well, I am not sure. There was always a rumor that she had a kid. I think it was a little girl. People saw them sometimes. When I asked her about it, she didn't answer me."

I sighed and said, "It seems like it would be hard to hide a child."

Janice agreed. "Not many of the gals hide their kids. Lou Ann seemed like an unlikely mother, but you know, to keep a kid hidden, going from place to place, she must have loved it. Otherwise she could have just dropped it off at a hospital. I mean, they take kids in."

"She was different, huh?"

"Yes, she was. She even dated Ben for a while."

"Ben from the restaurant?" I shouted by accident and Janice looked at me a little closer.

"Yes, honey, Ben. He and Nancy had split up. Nancy ran off with a loser for a while. So anyway, yeah, he fell for Lou Ann. He's one of the people who told me about the kid."

"Oh, so somebody met the kid. I wonder what happened to her?"

"Poor baby, God knows. Ben thought she was a cute kid, but he said she was really weird."

"Oh yeah?"

"Yeah, he said she was as quiet as a mouse and slipped around like a little ghost. He thought Lou Ann needed to put her in school so she could have a normal life. I think that's what ended it for them. Lou Ann just told him to fuck off."

"Was Ben sad?"

"For a short time. Nancy came back and then Lou Ann was gone, on the move. That was her deal. Always movin'."

"Did you think about turning her in for keeping that kid while she was a prostitute?"

"Ha! No way. I mean she loved the kid, I think. She always made money, so it wasn't for me to judge. If I thought she let the kid get hurt or roughed up, I would have done something. I don't know what, though. What would you have done?"

I tried not to look shocked, but Janice noticed my discomfort and said, "It doesn't matter, though, does it? Lou Ann's dead and hopefully the kid is okay."

I took a deep breath and said, "I probably would have wanted to see the child. Then I could decide. Maybe she was lonely and just needed some friend or maybe didn't know what she wanted because she was trapped in Lou Ann's world." My lip quivered, and my voice shook. Janice took my hand and said, "Oh, honey, we've hit a nerve here. Let's not talk about this anymore. I am so sorry."

"It's okay. I have a soft spot for children, that's all." I managed a smile and thought, you have got to deal with this shit, Leah.

Chapter 43

Carl

Letting Leah go was hard. I wanted to trust. I wanted to believe she would be okay. I tried to keep my fears from her. It was harder than she knew. She was not Lou Ann. I had learned that in the years she was with us. She had an innocence about her. Even though she had lived a hard and strange life, her lack of exposure to normalcy worried me.

But what was normal? No doubt Sharon and I lived a kind of steady life, but we were not from typical families. Our pasts were bumpy and twisted and full of dark corners. We managed to live with everything that had come before we met each other, but it was all always there, lurking in the shadows.

Leah was a gift I didn't want to let go of. We kept in touch, and we saw her often enough, but her quest worried me. What would she find but heartache? Lou Ann should not have kept her. Leah's family is a total mystery. And then, there are the people up and down the coastline who knew Lou Ann. Most were bad in some way. She could stumble into things, thinking she would find a piece of herself and instead she would just find darkness.

Sharon was more trusting. She said Leah was tougher than I realized. She said Leah would find enough to soothe her longing and then move on. I was not so sure.

Then there was our last name, Moses. Sometimes I wanted to know more about where Earl and May came from. I wanted to understand Earl, but I didn't know if I could open that door and come out alive. As much as I believed I was more like May, I still felt his rage. I worried his shadow could overcome me if I got too close. It was like having a maniac locked in the basement and no one else knew he was there. One slip up, one urge acted on, and he would be in my world again.

When Lou Ann came back, I thought hard about how I could have killed Earl. How did I live with it and never go crazy? Who am I that I did it knowingly? Who am I that I persuaded May to help me? Was I Earl that day? Maybe Earl's brutality was part of me after all. I don't remember feeling much more than relief when the deed was done. That has to come from some pretty dark shit.

Seems everyone in this family had too many disconnects. None of us – Sharon, Lou Ann, Leah, me – knew enough about ourselves. It was some kind of curse. Lou Ann's death didn't change that at all. It just pushed it back in my face, full force

and added Leah's loss of connection too.

Chapter 44

Leah

I knew that it was possible I was going to remember things that I didn't want to remember. I realized that from the start, but I had to risk it. Bad memories might be gifts in disguise. They might free me. They might shed light on the dark terror that was just under the surface. I think I had a fantasy that some of those memories would be good ones, and I could balance myself against the good and bad. I pushed through, knowing they could hurt me, but I was so determined that something useful was there, so I just kept wandering and trying to see my past in the windows and sidewalks of the Oregon coast.

It was on one of my days off and I was reading an article in the paper about all the homeless people and how they got that way. The article was talking about the drugs, the mental illness, the unemployment that goes on for too long. I started to think about Lou Ann and myself and wondering if we were really homeless. Maybe we were not. We had a roof over our heads nearly every night and sometimes they were real rooms, real trailers. Lou Ann made money, and she really didn't take drugs, at least I never knew that she did. Even her beer drinking wasn't that bad. But she must have really fit the crazy part. She had to be nuts, right?

That afternoon while reading the paper I remembered one of our "homes" and what happened to me there. It had been right there behind me, waiting to emerge. I let down the wall, and it came in.

I think I was very young, maybe five. I was beginning to lose teeth. That happens when you are five. We were in some kind of abandoned building. I don't know what town we were in and I was not allowed to go out while we were there. I don't know how long it was, really; I have no concept. Maybe a few months…

The place was bad. There were rats and possums and the occasional raccoon. They were not cute. They would bite you, scratch you, hiss at you and take your food. It wasn't a Disney movie, I can tell you that.

We occupied a corner of the building. Lou Ann had pulled some machinery and miscellaneous garbage together to create a couple of walls. We had sleeping bags she had picked up at one of the shelters. We stuffed t-shirts into old pillow cases from the thrift store and used them for pillows. It wasn't summer, so we lived in layers of clothes. We had a small camp stove and we ate soup or canned spaghetti or whatever else Lou Ann brought in. We didn't wash much. I went through that time of my life without a full bath. I was cold and hungry a lot. We were in hiding, but I wasn't sure why.

Lou Ann was very quiet, and I was instructed to be silent at all times. In my weird upbringing I had never been encouraged to talk, so this was easier than you might think. I knew how to entertain myself for hours with whatever I could find. Lou Ann had trained me well. She didn't seem to be concerned with me doing anything wrong to call attention to us. She was preoccupied with worry. She paced around the building and smoked constantly. She ate very little, and I think that is why I was hungry then. Food was always something Lou Ann had to do, not something she wanted to do. Whatever was on her mind kept everything else out of her mind. She was not really there with me, and she was scared.

During this time, she would leave for a couple of days at a time. She would tell me when she was going and made sure I knew I was not to leave even if it took a little longer for her to get back. Most of the time she left me with enough food, but I was not allowed to use the stove while she was gone. To this day I cannot eat white bread and peanut butter. The thought of it makes me gag. I now realize it was all I lived on for about one week, maybe a little longer.

She had left when it was dark. She took a bag with her "working clothes" in it, and as she left, she turned back and looked at me for a long time. I don't remember what she said, but whatever it was made me realize she might be gone for a while. As I watched her climb out the window on the side of the building, I was afraid she might never come back for me. I sat down and cried silent tears.

I can see myself in my mind's eye. A little tiny girl with matted hair, a dirty face, dirty clothes, skinny as a rail. I see myself and I want to kill Lou Ann, but she is already dead.

The other people came within a few days. I was lying in my sleeping bag trying to stay warm, and I heard someone talking. There were two voices, both men. They were talking about getting more beer and arguing about who needed to go out and try to get it. I crept out of my bag and peeked through our "wall." They were sitting under the window Lou Ann had climbed out. They looked like any hoboes, but they had good boots and good packs. Lou Ann had told me that good boots and good packs meant they planned to stay on the road, nothing to lose and more dangerous. I held my breath.

But they saw me. One of them stood up and walked over and lifted me over the makeshift wall. I didn't fight him, still trying to be quiet. I went limp, and he dropped me to the ground. "What the hell is this kid doing in here? Hey, Jim, take a look at this."

His partner turned from the window and strode over to size me up. He touched me with the tip of his boot and said, "She is damn near dead!"

What happened next was terrifying. I realize now that it could have been much worse, but it was bad enough. First, they broke down our walls and scrounged to find anything of value. Nothing but half a loaf of white bread and a jar of peanut butter. They tore up whatever order we had managed to make of our corner. Then they were angry. All there was to steal was lousy food, no booze, and now they had a dirty brat (that is what they called me) to worry about. They decided to tie me up so I wouldn't run. They sat me on my sleeping bag with my hands and feet bound. I remember the rope cutting into my wrists, and when I whimpered, the one named Jim said he would cinch them up if I didn't shut up.

They sat there and contemplated what they might do. LeRoy wanted to take me to a hospital and drop me off at the emergency room late at night. Jim wasn't so sure I couldn't be sold to someone. LeRoy thought I wasn't worth much as far as money because I was too damn little to be of any use just yet, even if they sold me to "one of those weirdos that likes little kids." Jim thought I was probably "retarded" and my folks just left me here because they couldn't deal with it. "She hasn't said shit. She either can't talk or is retarded. She is useless, I guess."

LeRoy thought I might be able to beg for booze money for them, at least for a while, before someone picked me up. Jim reminded him, "We are in the goddamn USA, you idiot. This isn't Mexico. No one is going to let us do that." This conversation went on for what I think was a few days. They fed me the peanut butter sandwiches; they let me pee in our bucket, and they lay me down at night. They came and went a lot, always returning with something to drink. That was my first taste of beer. They didn't bother to get me anything else to drink. I thought it tasted like pee smelled, and I gagged when they poured it in my mouth.

They loved to get drunk. They talked about their life on the road: where they would go next, time in prisons, time in foster care, fathers that beat them, mothers who took piles of pills, women who cheated on them, cops that punched them. Pretty much everything awful had happened to these two. They ignored me mostly, but when I would come up in the conversation, I was terrified. Anything they said they would do sounded horrible. Once Jim said, "We could just kill her and put her out of her misery. She is retarded and abandoned, and we both know what they will do to her in a foster home. We could just hit her over the head and leave her in the bag." LeRoy thought someone was going to come back for me, maybe, and what if they came while they were still there. That is when they decided to move me so they could decide what to do next. They didn't want to risk any angry person returning to claim me.

The clarity of this memory was like a 3-D movie in my mind. I could hear it, feel it and remember how sick with fear I was. If they moved me, Lou Ann would never find me. I could not stop crying, silent tears. My heart was breaking; my arms were tired; my legs hurt; I was hungry, and now I would be lost. I would just stop being. I would die, and she would not be able to find me.

They put me in the sleeping bag, tied it up loosely. They put a gag in my mouth, just in case I tried something, and started walking. I don't know where we went or how long it took because I must have passed out. Next thing I remember is a lean-to by the ocean, under a bridge. Jim was sitting beside me, drinking out of a bottle. We were sitting between two big rocks on a little dirt platform. He was rambling on about LeRoy and how he had a big mouth and now we had to keep moving. He said, "I am not taking you with me. I don't care what he says. You are a pain in the ass, kid. Someone will find you; you will be okay…"

Then I saw Jim walking towards me with something in his hand and a mean look on his face. I think he hit me in the head with something to knock me out. I don't remember anything else but waking up in my sleeping bag, in a motel room, with Lou Ann sitting on the bed smoking Camels and drinking a glass of milk. I do remember that we didn't talk about what happened to me. She just said, "You need to rest, kid, and I will bring you some fried clams. Just go to sleep." End of story. I don't know how she found me, why Jim hit me, nothing. I don't even know if I have blocked out more, maybe worse. Like most of life, it isn't really mine, now is it?

Two drunks, stupid, used up and left with the pieces of what was once a life. I am lucky they didn't hurt me more.

When this memory pushed its way into my life, I was filled with rage. And of course, no one to scream at, punch, kick, or run down. Here I stood, alone with a sickening memory, and just like all of the shit that was part of my Lou Ann life, the person I could blame was gone.

Before this memory, sometimes I would be surrounded by people in the restaurants, on the street, on a boardwalk at the beach and I think I could disappear, just like Lou Ann taught me. But once I remembered LeRoy and Jim, all that power left me. I was laid bare, touchable, visible, and no way to control it but to stay away from people. This memory helped push me into the solitary confinement that would be my future.

I wanted to tell someone about it, so I called Sharon. I started to talk about it, and I just couldn't get it out of my mouth. I started sobbing. She said, "Write it down, honey. Just write it down and if you need to, burn it, or send it to me, or tear it up and let the wind carry it away. Just get it out of your head." I sat down and wrote this and now it is part of this story. You can decide for yourself what you think it did to me. Maybe you can decide how I ended back with Lou Ann. Maybe, but what does it matter? Same shit no matter how you dress it up.

If I had remembered it when I was with Lou Ann, I don't think I could have continued to be her silent little one. I believe I hid it so I could stay with her and pretend she could save me. But maybe that

isn't it at all. Maybe....

Chapter 45

Leah

Janice knocked on my trailer door. I answered, and she stood there with this uncomfortable sympathetic smile, and she said, "Go see Ben. I told him you are Lou Ann's kid." I opened my mouth to protest, and she turned and walked away. She had figured it out. I was too obvious. Damnit. Now Ben would just feel sorry for me. How could he be honest now? Goddamnit.

My first impulse was to pack up and leave. I kept my belongings fairly simple, just like Lou Ann taught me. I could pack up, move back to Carl and Sharon's for a while. Find a new job, maybe buy a car and then what?

I sat and stared at the linoleum, worn and peeling. I thought of all the lonely women and men who had sat here before. I imagined them all as runners. People who walked away: Lou Ann's. I looked at the shabby furniture and the water stained ceiling and wondered why I thought this was okay for me. I wasn't an old drunk or a used-up whore. I wasn't someone who hurt people and left them broken and bruised. I did not deserve to live in this crazy trailer in this shitty town, just because someone had dragged me through it when I was helpless and caged. I drank some whiskey, which I rarely did, and I smoked a joint and I rolled myself in pity. I screamed at the walls, and I cried bitter tears. I longed for a mother. I longed for a home. I longed for everything I didn't have, and then I passed out.

When I woke up I felt different, more than just hung over. The trailer felt cramped and smelled. The worn carpet made me gag, and I had to throw up over and over. I could smell other people in there, and the cigarettes and dirt made my head hurt. The sinks had rust stains, the shower was gross, and the windows let in the cold sea air. It was a dump, and I didn't need to live like this. I was not born to crawl up and down that coastline like a beggar.

Over the next few days I realized what I was trying to do, go back and find Lou Ann, was not the right way to go about things. I was hiding in the past. I didn't want to do it anymore. I had to take a different road. So, I changed my quest to understand Lou Ann and my childhood. I was going to make myself, not find myself. I was going to be more than the stray that Lou Ann dragged all over. I was going to stop the self-pity that had started to consume me and just "chuck it."

Tough words and tougher to make all that happen. Sometimes we wake up with a resolve to do things differently, and once in a blue moon it works. But most of the time it is just a dream and we fall back down to where we were before. Part of me did let go of the past after that, but the damage was done, and it was all going to be part of who I became. No escape, no resolution, no happy ending.

I called my favorite mother, Sharon and said, "I want to come home for a while."

Chapter 46

Leah

Before I went home to Carl and Sharon, I did go see Ben. We sat in the bar on the afternoon I was packed and ready to leave. Carl would be picking me up in a couple of hours. Ben sat across from me in his short sleeve shirt, hairy muscular arms on the table. He patted my hand and smiled. After I found out he was who he was, his face and his movements became more familiar to me.

He cleared his throat and started to speak. "Honey, I need to tell you I knew who you were as soon as you applied. I was so happy to see you looking well, and when Nelda called, I was thrilled to have you."

"Nelda told you about me?" I was stunned.

"The coast is not that big a place. And Big Betty's old man told her about you and, well, Carl and Sharon did too. So many people knew about you, Leah." He cleared his throat again. "I want to tell you I am sorry. I should have insisted you were taken away from Lou Ann. I just couldn't make myself do it. I was afraid, you know, that she would die without you."

He had tears in his eyes, and his voice shook. "You were so sweet, and I knew you weren't getting all you needed. I am just so sorry, Leah."

I was speechless. I just looked at him. I didn't know what to say. Lou Ann did die when she gave me up. She died, and I was still here. I was still alive, but my life was about Lou Ann. I was never me. Even Ben could not do the right thing for a little child because of her. I was not her, but she was my life. I felt empty, like nothing. Ben held my hand and said I was so lovely and well-mannered and la-di-da. But guess what, I wasn't Lou Ann, so what did it matter to him? Who was I but her stray, her pet, her crutch?

When I got up, I thanked Ben for the job and made my getaway. Halfway to my trailer, I saw Carl's pickup waiting to load me and my scooter up and take me back to the only home I'd ever had.

Chapter 47

Sharon

Carl had told me his truth in pieces. Maybe he couldn't say it all at once. It came out in bursts. It was a crap history: terrible to hear, worse to carry. Lou Ann should have been told the truth about her mother. It was her story, and no one should have kept it from her.

Earl and the murder was the greatest shock. I tried to image the hatred and fear that they all felt for that son of a bitch. For Lou Ann, it was life or death. She had to kill her captor. Maybe for May it was the same. But for Carl, it was all about the guilt.

Earl never hurt him like he did the women. He was tough and mean, but he never was brutal to him. Killing Earl was for his mother and his sister. Living with it, well, that was agony.

Once he told me that he looked like Earl, especially his build. Imagine if you put that big strong body into hurting tiny women? Carl was terrified of becoming like him.

But May was in Carl. He had the quiet strength, the open heart, the tendency to keep his thoughts to himself. He was her Boy Bear and she gave him her spirit. May gave Carl her loyalty, even the crazy loyalty she felt for Spring and keeping the truth from Lou Ann. The kind of loyalty that Carl still felt for Lou Ann, even when she pushed and clawed her way out of their lives. Even when she brought him a broken child with blue eyes like shattered glass who had been raised like a wildling. All that came from May and all that made him who he was, and it was better than Earl.

Chapter 48

Leah

When I returned to Sharon and Carl's, I was a different person. Now I was a woman and I wasn't the sweet little waif they first took into their lives. When I went in my old room (the same one I shared with Lou Ann; even my room was not all mine), I lay on the bed and stared at the ceiling, then the wall, then the carpet. I stayed pretty immobile for a few days. Sharon and Carl didn't push me. Sharon brought up a sandwich, a piece of cake, some milk, some roast, whatever she was making. She washed the clothes I brought back and made sure I had plenty of fresh towels. The house smelled wonderful, just like Sharon. It was fresh and clean; the windows sparkled, and the floors were shiny.

My mind was cluttered with new information and old feelings. I felt like I was a flimsy piece of paper, all see-through and blowing around in the wind. I couldn't latch onto anything but the tastes and smells that Sharon's home brought me.

I went back to when I was fourteen years old and Carl shared the stories of murdering Earl and Lou Ann's mother. These stories or confessions as you might call them were pieces of a puzzle that had no name. Was it the life of Carl Moses? Was it the life of Lou Ann the Lost Child? Was it connected to what was done to me? I went back to when I first came to Carl and Sharon's house. Maybe that would have been a good time to tell me about the murder, with Lou Ann there with us. But Lou Ann would never have stood for that, would she? What if she had known about her mother? Would it have made a difference in her choices? From what I knew of her, I think it might have helped her to know her mother loved her, but I am not so sure about that. All of it felt like Lou Ann got away, and I was left to carry her load, again. I could not escape. I was destined to keep living her life.

If I think of staying with Sharon and Carl again as a healing time, it makes sense to me. The couple of years on the coast, on my own, were more brutal than I had thought they were at the time. I was mining for gold and kept coming up with black coal. The past left me with some answers, but no understanding of why. I was digging into painful experiences and the cost to my psyche was high. Being alone all of that time only added to my crippling silence. It only made the nights darker and the cold colder. It didn't give me peace of mind. It didn't give me myself, my story. It took time to recover from that ordeal.

The weather took a turn for the worse after I had been home a week or two. There were huge lashing wind storms with driving rain. The days were dark, and we kept lights on all day. It brought me out of my room. I started exploring the books in the house again and spending time with Sharon. She let me lead on whatever topic I could handle at the time. Sometimes we went deep into the dark corners of my youth. Sometimes we talked about May and Earl and Spring. We wondered about Carl and how he had survived that childhood. We wondered if Spring would have changed her mind about Lou Ann staying at the House of Moses if she had met Earl. We were sure she would have taken Lou Ann back to her aunt. We wondered if I should go to college. We wondered if I should get a job.

These were good conversations. Sharon was the kind of person you could have a real conversation with. She listened, she probed when it was the right time, and she let you say whatever you wanted. Even when I said I hated Lou Ann, that I would never be okay, she didn't argue. She just listened and made me feel sane.

I spent some time with Carl, but I felt like Lou Ann was always in the room with us. I wanted him to myself, but that was not possible, she was always there in him. I wanted him to be my father, my friend, and my savior. But Lou Ann was a dark shadow that hung around him. She was a deep sigh he would make when he was tired. She was the way he pushed his hair out of his eyes and took a long drink of whiskey. She pushed her way into his life, and he was willing to let her occupy that space. I couldn't understand how Sharon took it, but she didn't talk about it, and I didn't ask. Such a good well-trained monkey was I.

When I watched Sharon move through the house and looked at her face when Carl recalled the past to me, I saw that she had made her own peace with Carl's history and with his present state of mind. I just didn't think I was as strong as Sharon. I just didn't think I could ever forgive a man for loving someone else. Where would I get that kind of strength?

Chapter 49

Sharon

My time in this story is coming to an end. I have no more to offer you, dear reader. I have loved a man named Carl, beautiful and strong. He came with a past and so did I. Our past lives stayed quiet and showed in our faces for only fleeting moments until Lou Ann came back. Then the past burst into the room like a wild stallion riding on the beach at full speed. I was caught up in more than the love of a little girl named Leah; I was dragged into the wind-whipped past of Lou Ann and Carl's childhood.

Leah and I were bystanders to their drama. We had our own dramas, our own loss, but the center of our world was them. We clung to each other for refuge, but our lives were twisted into theirs, and no matter how hard we fought back, we were caught up in the world of the Moses family.

I had come to terms with my past, but I had a solid past to come to terms with. Leah just had bits and pieces of a jagged past, rough and lonely, with no smooth edges to hold onto. I watched her rail against it, and I stood by and let her have her experience. I worried night and day that she would not find peace. I worried that the damage done had gone farther than we could imagine. Sadly, my worries became the reality. The damage had gone too far. She would not be "all right." She would just "be," like most of us. She would not become a wonderful mother, a lover, a sister, a friend. Those things were beyond her reach. Those were dreams for other women. She was left on the shore to ponder, never able to take that swim into the exhilarating and terrifying surf. Stranded on the shore, smelling the salt air, feeling the wind and longing for connection.

I will let Leah tell you what became of her...

The Wreckage

Chapter 50

Leah

When I came back to live with Carl and Sharon I was developing into an angry person. My search into the past only made me feel that I was less, always less than Lou Ann. No one saved me, because they loved a wild and unhinged prostitute who roamed the coast. Beautiful but brutal, hard as steel, always moving, one little girl forced to trail behind her. Everyone turned their heads. Everyone let her keep me. I hated everyone but Sharon. Carl's confessions made me hate him too – not right away but after a while. He even murdered for her. She cast her spell on him, and it was a life sentence.

I withdrew to the ocean. Every day I walked for miles. I was already lean, and I became very strong. I spent hours with the wind in my face, my footprints going south, then north. The constant sound of pounding surf in my ears. Rain was no obstacle. I had good rain gear. Sun, well I had sunscreen. I cut my hair short for the first time so I could pull on a watchman's cap or a hood and not worry. My face was always tanned. Sharon said my eyes were more beautiful than ever. It did not matter to me.

Those words only made me think, if I was so beautiful, why didn't she bring me to Carl and Sharon sooner? Why didn't anyone care enough? Beauty had not saved me. It never would, and I would not allow it.

My pity party was lonely. I did not share it with anyone. No one really knew what I was thinking. Carl and Sharon knew I was hurting, but they did not interfere. I had no one who could look at me and see anything or anyone but Lou Ann. I hated her for all those days. My walking was the only way I could manage my feelings. The little girl who always had to hide and be silent. Now I pushed those feelings into the wind. I spat them into the surf, and I fought them with every footprint in the sand. Hard work, that is what it was, hard work.

Sometimes the release was devastating. When Uncle Carl told me about Spring and the truth about where Lou Ann came from and why she ended up with the Moses family, he did it to make things clearer. I was still only a kid. But now, it just muddied the waters for me. Maybe, just maybe, Lou Ann might have been able to connect with someone if she knew she came from someone who was kind and good. Maybe she would have chosen differently. They robbed Lou Ann of her story, and then she robbed me of mine.

Maybe May and Carl could have saved her from Earl. Why didn't they? It sounds like Earl would have lived on if not for Lou Ann's prompting them to kill him. How long were they going to stand by? Why didn't they all leave him? Why did they just watch him destroy her?

And hey, she had some kind of roots. They could even be traced. But Lou Ann in her selfishness left me with none. What city did she find me in? Why didn't she find my mother's name? Why didn't she try, even for the smallest piece of my life? Fucking bitch. I must have repeated that in my mind a hundred times. Fucking selfish, no-good, rotten piece-of-shit bitch.

What could life have been if she had brought me as a baby to Carl and Sharon? Sharon was a natural mother. She was my fairy godmother, but even she could not erase what I knew, what I saw and how it left me. She loved me completely and without conditions, and it was good, but it could not lift my burdens. Even Carl still saw Lou Ann. He still had pain and longing in his face. It would never leave. That was what Lou Ann could do to a life. Sharon was patient with him, but she never indulged him. She remained steady for all of us.

The worst of my "days of wreckage" subsided, and I moved on. Carl and Sharon had watched me, but they did not interfere. Carl wanted to get me a dog to walk with me, but I said no. This is my own journey.

There was the part of me that knew I had to make a way for myself and I have done that. I went to college and realized I was not only pretty (since so many people liked to tell me that) but very intelligent and I was able to grasp anything I put my hand to. I chose accounting. It was a cold and number-driven profession. I did not have to connect; in fact, I didn't even have to meet the people I worked for. I could earn money, work at home and take care of myself.

There have been times I was tempted to try and create a friendship here or there. But all the filters had been lifted from my eyes because of the childhood I could not escape. I did not see a man and imagine a family, a house, two kids, love. I saw a man. I saw that look I had seen in Bernie's eyes, lust and wanting. I knew that I would be the delivery system for any man I let into my world and I was not going to let that happen.

When I met a woman and I thought maybe I was interested in knowing more about her, I remembered how it felt when Amy left. I didn't think I could handle a casual friendship. What if I just kept falling in love with women, and they just kept leaving? Or what if they stayed, how could I explain my life to them? No, it is better to stay single, just Leah.

I will carry the loss of connection with me forever. I am a strange woman. I am a stranger in my own life, a person removed. People still tell me I am beautiful, but I never feel joy from that. I have never had a man or a woman that I wanted to love, except for Amy.

When I finished college, I moved to the coast, not too far from Carl and Sharon, but far enough. I bought property and built a simple one-story house with a view of the Pacific. I found work that paid enough to live in comfort. My house is clean, small, with straight lines and big windows. It is uncluttered, and the tiles shine on my kitchen floor. I have a plant or two for the air quality. May's drawings are on the wall, but Lou Ann's urn did not come here with me. My small sea shrine is on my deck, beside my chair and table.

Nothing is out of place. I never plan to leave. I never want to share it.

My clothes are plain, and I keep my hair short. I eat only fresh food – no meat – clean, whole food. I don't drink or smoke, and I never use drugs. I just don't want them in my life. I will never abuse my body or let anyone else do that to me. I will remain untouched, clean, and singular.

I walk for miles every week along the coastline. That has never changed. I stay fit and I work hard.

I still don't have a dog, but a yellow cat adopted me, and she is allowed to sleep on the cushion in my rocker. Sometimes she walks on the beach with me, but she turns back long before I am ready.

Someday I will die, and someone will send my ashes to the ocean. I will roll in the waves with Lou Ann, May and Spring. Who knows, maybe my own lost mother is there too. Maybe she is in the waves that pound on the shore each day. Maybe she is in the spray of the surf that hits my face on windy days. Maybe she is in my eyes and my hair, and maybe she loved me at first. Maybe she did not know that the drugs had taken her. Maybe someone stole me from her, someone named Lou Ann. All these things and more will remain my mystery, my life.

THE END

Acknowledgements

Although I have been writing stories all of my life, whether it was in my head or on paper, I never endeavored to write a book until I was 60 years old. I could not have completed this book without the help of my husband Joe, my sisters Kay, Jill, Penny, and Susan, my niece Leslie and my dear friend Lynda. They helped push me along, even when I thought that it was not worth it. They encouraged me and provided insight about what they wanted to hear about my characters.

My editor was a saving grace. Without Margaret, I would still be trying to figure out if it was worth finishing or not. She gave me great encouragement and guidance and slashed and burned where I needed the help.

I hope you enjoy this tale. The characters are not based on any individuals, living or dead. They come from my skills of observation and my overactive imagination. Now I am ready to do it again.

Made in the USA
San Bernardino, CA
31 July 2018